DREAMWORKS
PENGUINS
of MADAGASCAR

MOVIE NOVELIZATION

adapted by Tracey W[...]

Simon Spotlight
New York London Toronto Sy[...]

This book is a work of fiction. Any references to historical events, real people, or real places are used fictitiously. Other names, characters, places, and events are products of the author's imagination, and any resemblance to actual events or places or persons, living or dead, is entirely coincidental.

SIMON SPOTLIGHT
An imprint of Simon & Schuster Children's Publishing Division
1230 Avenue of the Americas, New York, New York 10020
First Simon Spotlight paperback edition October 2014
Penguins of Madagascar © 2014 DreamWorks Animation L.L.C.
All rights reserved, including the right of reproduction in whole or in part in any form.
SIMON SPOTLIGHT and colophon are registered trademarks of Simon & Schuster, Inc.
For information about special discounts for bulk purchases, please contact
Simon & Schuster Special Sales at 1-866-506-1949 or business@simonandschuster.com.
Manufactured in the United States of America 0914 OFF
10 9 8 7 6 5 4 3 2 1
ISBN 978-1-4814-3728-8
ISBN 978-1-4814-3729-5 (eBook)

CHAPTER 1
Stop That Egg!

In the not-too-distant past . . .

Skipper. Kowalski. Rico. Private. They are penguins, but more than penguins. They are an elite unit. Soldiers. Heroes. Saving penguins who have been kidnapped from zoos and aquariums all over the world from bad guys. But like other heroes before them, these penguins came from humble beginnings. They were hatched in the frozen waste-land of Antarctica, where they waddled and played with the rest of the young penguins.

In those days, it was just Skipper, Kowalski, and Rico. When they weren't frolicking, they spent endless hours marching in long lines. Luckily, a documentary crew was there to capture it all on film.

"Does anyone even know where we're marching to?" young Skipper asked his friends.

Four adult penguins waddled past them.

"Who cares?" asked the first one.

"I question nothing!" announced the second.

"Me too!" added the third.

"Me too!" finished the fourth.

But Skipper *did* care. There had to be more to life than marching in line. He craned his neck to look up ahead, but all he could see were more penguins.

"Well, fine," Skipper said. "We'll just fly to the front of the line and see for ourselves. Kowalski, Rico, engage aerial surveillance!"

The two penguins stood on their tiptoes, flapping their short wings as hard as they could. Kowalski grunted. Rico's face turned red from the effort. But they didn't budge.

"Skipper, we appear to be flightless!" Kowalski reported.

Skipper held up his flippers.

"Well, what's the point of these?" he asked angrily.

Rico, the silent member of the group, looked thoughtfully at one of his flippers. Then he slapped one of Skipper's flippers with it in a high-five.

Skipper's eyes widened.

"Whoa! I like it!" he exclaimed. "Hey, this could be our thing! What are we gonna call it? Let's call it the, uh . . . the high-*one*!"

Suddenly a large white egg rolled into the penguins, knocking them over. It rolled away as they got back on their feet.

"Hey! Anybody see that? That's an egg! Is someone gonna go and get it?" Skipper yelled.

The nearest adult penguins stopped. They looked at one another nervously. "We can't do that," one replied.

"Well, why not?" Skipper asked.

"It's a dangerous world out there," another penguin explained. "And we're just penguins. You know, nothing but . . . cute and cuddly."

"Yeah, why do you think there are always documentary crews filming us?" a penguin asked.

Another penguin shrugged. "Sorry, kid. We lose

a few eggs every year. It's just nature."

"Right, nature. I guess that makes sense," Skipper replied, but then his eyes narrowed with steely determination. "Something . . . something deep down in my gut tells me that it makes no sense at all. You know what? I reject nature!"

The penguin marchers gasped loudly. Skipper raised a flipper like he was leading a charge in battle.

"Who's with me?" he yelled. "Ya-ha!"

He took off after the egg, sliding on his belly across the slippery ice. The egg launched right over a cliff! Skipper tried to stop, but he was going too fast. He slid headfirst off the cliff!

Then he suddenly stopped. Craning his neck, he saw that Kowalski and Rico had grabbed his feet and were pulling him back.

Skipper hopped to his feet and the three penguins peered over the cliff's edge. The egg was still furiously rolling down the cliffside, dodging sharp spikes of ice.

"Gah!" said Skipper, Kowalski, and Rico.

Then the egg landed on a ledge of soft snow,

and the penguins breathed a sigh of relief.

But the ledge broke off!

"Gah!" said the penguins again.

The snow tumbled farther down the cliff with the egg in the center, forming a giant snowball as it rolled. At the bottom of the cliff, the snowball hit the bow of an old abandoned whaling ship. It cracked in half.

"Gah!" cried the three young birds.

Unharmed, the egg spilled out onto the ship's deck.

"The old ship!" Kowalski exclaimed. "No one's ever returned from there alive."

"Relax, Kowalski, there's a bird down there now," Skipper told him. "Look, he's fine."

A tiny bird hopped across the ship when suddenly a huge leopard seal emerged from the water. It opened its tooth-filled mouth and swallowed the bird whole!

The penguins shrunk back in horror.

"Leopard seals!" Skipper growled. "Nature's snakes!"

"Aren't snakes nature's snakes?" Kowalski asked.

"How should I know?" Skipper asked. "I live on the flippin' frozen tundra!"

They watched as the huge seal climbed onto the ship's deck, followed by two other seals. They wriggled their way toward the helpless egg.

"They're going for the egg!" Skipper cried. "Gimme a way down there, ASAP!"

Kowalski thoughtfully stroked his chin with his flipper. "All one would have to do is collect thirty feet of kelp . . . ," he mused out loud.

The penguins didn't notice, but the film crew was right behind them. The director narrated in a whisper.

"Tiny and helpless, the baby penguins are frozen with fear. They know if they fall from this cliff, they will surely die." He nodded to his cameraman. "Gunter, give them a shove."

". . . harnessing the jellyfish we've trained to obey simple voice commands—" Kowalski was saying, when a microphone pole reached out and bumped into the penguins. The three of them tumbled down the cliffside.

"Now that's more like it!" Skipper cheered.

CHAPTER 2
Private Hatches

Still in the not-too-distant past . . .

They spilled onto the deck of the ship. Rico sailed forward, his arms ready to grab hold of the egg.

"Attaboy, Rico! Don't let those seals have it!" Skipper yelled.

Rico swept in just before the seals reached the egg. He picked it up—and popped it into his mouth, swallowing it in his miraculous gullet.

"Okay, I guess that works," Skipper said.

Now the seals noticed the penguins. They lunged forward, snapping at their flippers.

"Get to higher ground!" cried Kowalski.

The three penguins grabbed onto a rope attached to a harpoon gun that looked like a long metal spear. They swung themselves on top of the gun and out of the seals' reach.

"Boo-yah!" Skipper cheered.

But the weight of the penguins caused the harpoon gun to dip, and they started to slide right to the seals.

"I'd recommend firing it now," Kowalski said.

"Nope. Hold on," Skipper ordered.

"Uh, we really should fire it," Kowalski repeated.

"Not till we see the whites of their eyes," Skipper insisted. That just seemed like the right thing to do.

Kowalski was starting to panic. "They're mostly pupil, very little white. Almost none!"

"They got to have a little bit of white, right?" Skipper asked.

Kowalski shook his head. "None whatsoever."

"What if they look really far to the left?" Skipper pressed.

Snap! A massive set of jaws clamped down inches away from Skipper.

"Fire in the hole!" Skipper yelled.

Rico pulled the trigger, and the long harpoon shot from the gun, carrying the three penguins with it. They arced across the water and landed one on top of the other on the surface of an iceberg. The egg popped out of Rico's beak.

They had done it! They'd saved the egg!

"Kowalski, analysis?' Skipper asked.

"We are really awesome at this!" Kowalski replied.

Skipper's eyes got wide as he realized something. "Hey! Hey! We can do our thing!" he said. "High-one!" He held up a flipper, and they all smacked flippers. It felt good.

Smack! Smack! Smack! They kept doing it. In his excitement, Skipper accidentally smacked the egg, and it began to crack.

"Oops. My bad," Skipper said.

They heard a pecking sound, and the egg cracked some more.

"Look, it's the miracle of birth," Skipper said.

Splat! The egg cracked all the way open, spewing goo all over them.

"Ick! That's disgusting!" Skipper wailed.

A chick popped out. His skin was wrinkly and damp from the fluid inside the egg. The top of the eggshell was stuck to his head. He had a goofy grin on his baby face. It was newly hatched Private!

"*Aaaah!*" The penguins recoiled.

But Private smiled at them, and they couldn't help smiling back.

"Hello! Are you my family?" the little guy asked.

The three penguins looked around them. The iceberg was floating far away from their home in Antarctica. They were surrounded by ocean on all sides—an ocean filled with leopard seals, sharks, and other creatures that loved to eat penguins.

"You don't have a family, and we're all going to die," Kowalski answered.

Private's lip quivered. Skipper slapped Kowalski.

"Nobody's gonna die!" he said firmly.

He pulled the eggshell off the baby's head.

"You know what you've got, kid? You've got us. And we've got each other," Skipper told him. "If that ain't a family, I don't know what is."

He saluted Private, who adorably saluted him back. Skipper tousled the feathers on his head.

"Kowalski, what's our trajectory?"

Kowalski held up a flipper and looked at the sun.

"Ninety-five percent certain, we're still doomed," he reported.

"And, uh, the other five percent?" Skipper asked.

"Adventure and glory like no penguins have ever seen before!" Kowalski replied.

Skipper nodded. "I'll take that action."

"Where are we going?" Private asked.

"The future, boys. The glorious future," Skipper replied as the iceberg sailed into the sunset.

CHAPTER 3
Happy Birthday, Private!

Ten years later . . .

A funky beat pumped throughout the Afro Circus tent.

"Afro Circus! Afro Circus! Polka dot, polka dot, polka dot . . ."

Normally the penguins worked security backstage while their zoo friends performed for the excited crowds. But tonight, they were on a mission.

Rico lit a long fuse outside the circus tent. As the fuse burned, it snaked around the tent and then curved into the entrance.

Rico followed the burning fuse. It burned past Private, who was dancing to the beat. Skipper stood by the circus's colorful cannon, taking it all in.

"Kowalski, status report!" he barked.

"I am *really* getting tired of this song!" Kowalski replied.

He ran up to the cannon, carrying a rolled-up circus banner. Rico jumped beside him and together they stuffed the banner inside the mouth of the cannon. Then Kowalski and Rico jumped in, followed by Skipper and Private.

Skipper grinned. "That's the best part of owning a circus. You can transport a cannon over state lines."

Boom! They shot from the cannon through the top of the circus tent. The circus banner unfurled to become a crude glider, and the four penguins held on tightly as they soared across the night sky.

"Ten years ago, on this very day, a tiny egg hatched, and our world got a little bit cuter," Skipper said, and Private giggled.

"So tonight, Private, we celebrate your birthday by infiltrating the United States Gold Depository in Fort Knox, Kentucky!" Skipper announced.

"Splendid!" Kowalski cheered.

Rico beamed happily.

"What?" Private asked, alarmed.

Down below, the huge fortress came into view. Guard towers surrounded the building, as well as a concrete wall topped with razor wire.

Skipper's eyes gleamed. "The Royal Flush."

"Skipper . . . ," Private said nervously.

Skipper shot him a warning glare. "Private, what's our rule about interrupting analogies?" he asked.

"Sorry, please continue," Private said.

Skipper sighed. "The moment's gone. Private ruined it!"

"Sir, we're approaching our target," Kowalski warned.

Bam! They smashed into a wall on the top of Fort Knox. Quickly recovering, they peered over the edge of the roof. Two military police officers stood guard at the entrance.

Private was not liking this at all. "But, Skipper, I really don't—"

"Are you questioning my leadership, Private?" Skipper asked.

"No, sir!" Private said quickly.

"Too bad," Skipper said. "'Cause I respect a soldier with some moxie."

"Really?" Private asked hopefully. "Then I really think we shouldn't—"

Skipper held up his flippers. "Whoa, whoa, whoa! Dial back the moxie, sass mouth."

Private pouted, and Skipper ruffled the feathers on Private's head. "Aw, look at you! Still so adorable."

Private sighed. Would Skipper ever take him seriously?

Skipper continued with the plan. He motioned to Rico, who tossed him a toy with a spinning clock face. He threw the toy off the roof and ducked back down.

"Fire in the hole!" he yelled.

The toy landed between the two military police officers. The arrow on the clock face stopped spinning and landed on the number eight.

"Eight o'clock. Night-night time!" the toy

announced in a mechanical voice.

Pssshhhht! A cloud of knockout gas sprayed from the toy and created a cloud around the two policemen. They dropped to the ground, unconscious.

After the gas thinned out, the penguins dropped down in front of the entrance. Private looked around nervously.

"Private! Come on!" Skipper hissed.

Inside the entry hall, more guards patrolled. But Skipper had it figured out. A black-and-white loading dock crossed over the entrance. The penguins used natural camouflage to pass over it. They lay belly-up on the white tiles, so their white bellies blended in. On the black tiles, they flipped face-down. The guards didn't notice them and they quickly reached the door of the vault.

"Please enter the passcode," a smooth computer voice instructed.

"Kowalski, you're on," Skipper said.

"Please enter the passcode."

Holding out a flipper, Kowalski turned to Rico. "Sonic incursion device."

Rico coughed up a cassette tape recorder into Kowalski's flipper. He held it up to the speaker's electronic lock and pressed play. A fiddle tune erupted from the speaker.

Skipper raised an eyebrow. "Oh, come on. Really?"

"We're in Kentucky, Skipper," Kowalski reminded him. "They do love their fiddle music."

Clunking sounds came from the massive vault lock as it started to open. *Y'all come in now, ya hear? Get yourself an iced tea,"* the computer voice said. The doors opened, bathing them in golden light. Skipper entered first, leading the crew into a majestic space filled with rows and rows of golden bricks.

"Private, if you could have anything you wanted in the whole world, what would it be?" Skipper asked him.

"Well, gee, Skipper," Private said thoughtfully. "I think to be a meaningful and valued member of the team."

"Oh," Skipper said. "Well, we got you something else."

He led them past the gold into the Fort Knox break room and stopped in front of a huge vending machine.

"A vending machine?" Private asked.

"Not just *any* vending machine, Private," Skipper told him. "The last remaining home for those succulent but chemically hazardous bits of puffed heaven called . . ."

Private's eyes got wide as he noticed the packages inside the machine, glowing under the fluorescent light.

"Cheezy Dibbles!" he cried happily.

Skipper held up a coin. "Happy ding-dong birthday, ya little scamp."

Private took the coin, squealed with delight, and planted a grateful kiss on Skipper's cheek. Then he squeezed Kowalski in a bear hug before rushing over to Rico. Rico picked him up and planted a kiss right on his beak.

"Now hit that machine and get your present!" Skipper ordered Private.

Private giddily waddled up to the machine and made his selection. Skipper turned to face Kowalski and Rico.

"We just broke into the most secure facility in North

America. Do you know what that means?" he asked.

"We're wanted criminals who'll be on the lam for the rest of our lives, always feeling the hot breath of Johnny Law on our necks?" Kowalski asked.

"No!" Skipper replied. "It means that as elite units go, we're the elite-est of the elite. Top shelf in the bureau. The penultimate . . . plus one!"

Behind him, the bag of Cheezy Dibbles slid off the spiral rack. Just as it fell, two long octopus tentacles snaked out of the machine! They grabbed Private and sucked him inside!

Skipper turned around to address Private—but he was gone.

"Where'd Private go?" Skipper asked.

They approached the machine and saw Private trapped inside.

"Oh, there he is. D3," Kowalski said.

Skipper sighed. "Aw, Private. How much is he?"

"He's three dollars and fifty cents," Kowalski replied.

"Well, that's outrageous!" Skipper complained. "Even for Private!"

Fwip! A tentacle pulled Rico inside.

"Sir! The machine's alive!" Kowalski cried.

Fwip! A tentacle pulled him in next.

Skipper glared angrily at the machine. "I don't think I like your attitude, vending machine. Or your prices! Release them!"

Another tentacle slid out, and Skipper tried to grasp it, but it sucked him inside too.

A guard walked in, only to see the vending machine, stuffed with penguins, rise up on six octopus tentacles.

"What the . . . ?" the guard asked.

Bam! The machine head-butted him and crashed out of the break room.

It raced through the halls of Fort Knox, swinging from pipes and ceiling beams to avoid the guard. It swung higher and higher until . . . *smash!* It crashed right through the roof!

Then it launched itself upward into the sky. A helicopter appeared, releasing a giant metal claw hook.

Chunk! The hook grabbed onto the machine, and the helicopter flew off into the night.

CHAPTER 4
Dave

The helicopter flew all the way to Venice, Italy, a charming city of brick buildings with canals running through it. The copter hovered over a submarine parked at a dock and then lowered the vending machine onto the sub's deck.

The machine descended through a hatch and the walls fell apart, revealing a cage with the four penguins trapped inside. They were all coated with orange Cheezy Dibble dust.

"Kowalski, analysis," Skipper said.

"All evidence indicates," he began as his stomach rumbled loudly, "that I ate too many Cheezy Dibbles."

Private coughed, and a cloud of orange dust poofed out of his mouth.

"We're behind enemy lines and incredibly thirsty," Skipper said. "Rico, bust us out of this delicious prison."

Rico hacked up a paper clip, bent it, and picked the lock on the cage. The four penguins burst out and struck ready-to-fight poses.

"Nice work, Rico," Skipper said. "You are a meaningful and valued member of this team."

Meaningful and valued. Private sighed when he heard those words. Skipper had never said that about him. What would it take to impress him, like the others always did?

Private took the paper clip from the lock and tossed it down his gullet. He tried to cough it up, just like Rico, but he couldn't. Instead, he coughed and sputtered.

Skipper spun around and said, "Private! Quit lollygagging . . . and regular gagging."

Private swallowed the paper clip, wincing. "Sorry," he said.

Skipper looked around. "Dark and ominous. Two of my least favorite traits in a room," he said.

Then Private noticed something. "Oh, look! A button!"

He pressed a button on the floor, and the platform they were standing on lowered them into another room.

Skipper shook his head. "Private, what have I told you about—"

"Sorry, what?" Private asked, pressing another button.

A rumbling shook the room. A giant laser came down from the ceiling and pointed directly at the penguins.

"It looks like some sort of giant laser sent to kill us all, sir," Kowalski reported helpfully.

Skipper slid out of the laser's path. Private spotted the laser controls and scurried over.

"Ooh! Another button!" he cried.

"Nooo!" wailed Skipper, Kowalski, and Rico.

They dashed over to Private, stopping him before he could press it. And in the very next moment . . .

Drip. Drip. Drip.

Water slowly splashed down on them from above.

"Naughty, naughty." The penguins heard a creepy voice.

They looked up to see a mysterious figure on the catwalk above them. He wore a lab coat and had a weird, enormous head. But that wasn't the only weird thing about him—he was walking upside down, defying gravity!

"Pretty birds belong in their cages," the creepy guy cooed.

He jumped from the catwalk and landed in front of them in a tangled heap. His arms and legs were bent at impossible angles. The penguins made faces as he put them back into place.

"Ew!" they cried.

"Now, that's just hurtful," said the guy. "And I was so happy to see you again, Skipper, Kowalski, Rico, and sweet little Private."

He poked Private's beak. "Boop!"

"Who *are* you?" Skipper asked.

"The humans know me as Dr. Octavius Brine:

renowned geneticist and cheese enthusiast," he replied, advancing menacingly on the penguins. "But you know me by a different, much older name. A name perhaps you'd hoped you'd never hear again. A phantom. A shadow of a former life."

He paused dramatically. "I! AM! DAAAVE!" he cried, and a hideous purple octopus burst forth from the costume of Dr. Brine.

The penguins stared blankly at him.

"Kowalski?" Skipper asked.

"Sorry, sir. No clue," Kowalski reported.

"DAAAVE!" the octopus repeated.

"Daaave?" Kowalski asked.

"Daaave," said Dave the octopus.

"Dave?" asked Skipper.

"Daaave," said Dave.

"Dave?" asked Private.

"Daaave," Dave said again.

Rico shrugged as if to say, "Daaave?"

"You seriously don't remember me?" Dave asked.

Skipper tried to cover things up. "Dave! Dave! Right! Ah, yeah, long time! Uh, how's the wife?"

Dave was furious. "I've never been married!" he sputtered. His bulgy eyes narrowed menacingly. "You may not remember me, but I could never forget you. . . ."

He moved to a shelf lined with snow globes from different zoos around the world. He reached for one with a tentacle: the New York City Zoo. He shook it, making the snow fall inside.

"New York City," Dave began. "I was taken to the zoo there. Life was good. Roomy tank, great location, monkey house views."

The penguins nodded. They knew it well.

"I knew it would take time for people to appreciate my talents," Dave said, his mind wandering back to those days. He had wiggled his tentacles masterfully. He'd stuffed his whole body into a jar. People loved seeing him. Kids thought he was cool.

Dave glared at the penguins. "And then you arrived. You took everything from me. Four adorable penguins! With you around, no one wanted an old octopus anymore."

To make room for the penguins, Dave's tank had

been removed from the zoo. He'd been shipped out to another zoo. But once again, people only wanted to see the adorable penguins.

"And so it went, over and over, at zoo after aquarium," Dave went on. "Adorable penguins stole the show, while I was shunned. Forgotten. Unwanted. Alone."

Private wiped a tear from his eye. "That sounds awful."

"Oh, it was," Dave assured him. "I came to realize that some creatures are born to get all the love. The rest of us get nothing."

Behind him, Rico swallowed the entire row of globes. Dave turned just as Rico gulped down the last one.

"Ugh! What is wrong with you?" Dave asked.

Rico shrugged.

Skipper tried to smooth things over. "Oh Daryl, Daryl, Daryl, you can't blame us for what happened to you."

"Uh, *can*!" Dave said. "That's how this whole revenge thing works!"

He held up a canister of glowing green goo.

"And with this, I finally have the power to destroy you," he announced.

"Crikey!" exclaimed Private.

Dave snapped one of his tentacles and three octopus henchmen appeared.

"Nicholas, cage them!" he ordered one of them.

"I have bad news for you, Dennis," Skipper informed him. "You messed with the wrong birds. Because we are an elite unit; the best of the best. Cream of the corn on a platinum cob. And we're gonna take your deadly green goop and sashay right out of the exit hatch."

"And just how are you going to do that?" Dave asked.

"Deploy secret weapon!" Skipper commanded.

Skipper jumped on top of Private. Kowalski jumped on top of Skipper. Rico jumped on top of Kowalski, who squeezed Rico's belly. A cloud of orange Cheezy Dibble dust sprayed into the eyes of Dave and his henchmen.

"Ahh! The cheese! It burns!" Dave screamed.

28

He dropped the canister. The penguins, still stacked one on top of the other, jumped on the canister. Then they rolled across the floor to the elevator platform.

"Roll out!" Skipper yelled.

When they reached the platform, Skipper kicked the canister up to Rico. Rico swallowed it, and the boys escaped out of the hatch.

Dave growled, wiping the dust out of his eyes.

"After them!" he yelled.

CHAPTER 5
Gondola Chase!

The four penguins emerged onto the deck of the submarine. Gondolas—flat-bottomed boats steered by a gondolier rowing with a long oar—floated past them. People used them to get around the city.

"Taxi!" Skipper called out.

The nearest gondola held a couple staring into each other's eyes, and a guitarist playing romantic music. The penguins jumped in and tossed the couple and the gondolier out.

Skipper turned to the guitarist. "How about some music? Something chasey!"

The musician started playing a fast tune. Private looked back and saw the three octopus henchmen leaving the sub.

"Here they come!" Private yelled.

"Let's move!" Skipper urged.

Private and Rico each picked up an oar, and they paddled furiously through the canal. *Slam!* They banged into another gondola.

The gondolier shouted at them in Italian as they rowed away. Behind them, the octopi swam through the water and then hijacked a gondola. They used the gondolier like a puppet, making his arms row faster and faster as they chased the penguins.

"We've got baddies at six o'clock!" Private yelled.

"Kowalski, battle formation!" Skipper ordered.

Kowalski hopped up onto the stern of the ship, and Skipper hopped onto his shoulders. The octopi moved the gondolier's arms into a fighting stance. Skipper held out an oar, ready to battle.

"Ha! So you squeegees want to do the gondola mambo? Well, let's dance!"

Squirt! One of the octopi squirted ink into Skipper's eye. "Ow! Mother of pearl, that stings!" Skipper yelled. "I've lost visual! Kowalski! Be my eyes!"

"Uh, left!" Kowalski instructed him.

Skipper swung his oar wildly, and clocked the poor gondolier right in the head.

"Right! Right!" Kowalski urged.

Skipper swung and missed the octopi again, hitting the gondolier once more. The octopi took a swing at Skipper.

"Duck!" Kowalski cried.

Skipper ducked. The oar missed Skipper and smashed into a nearby window. An angry man swung open the window, knocking the octopi and the gondolier into the water.

"I think I got 'em," Skipper said, his eyes still filled with ink.

"They're down, sir!" Kowalski reported.

But then the octopi emerged from the water. Two of them stretched out and linked tentacles, forming an octopus slingshot. They catapulted the third octopus across the water.

"Skipper!" Kowalski warned.

"Go all terrain!" Skipper commanded.

The four penguins planted their oars onto the street. Still in the gondola, they held onto the oars and used them like stilts to pass through an outdoor café.

The octopi weren't far behind. They squeezed through a sewer grate flowing underneath the café and burst out of manhole covers on the ground. One octopus reached up and snatched Skipper's oar away from him.

"We've lost engine one!" Skipper cried.

Another octopus grabbed the oars away from Kowalski and Rico.

"And two and three!" Kowalski reported.

The third octopus grabbed Private's oar.

"Four!" Private announced. The gondola fell forward—and in an amazing stroke of luck, landed right on a scooter.

"Switch to emergency power!" Skipper commanded.

Private hopped onto the throttle of the scooter. "Aye-aye, Skipper!"

They turned into a dead end, where a merchant

33

was loading watermelons into a truck.

"We've got melons! Dead ahead!" Private called out.

Rico acted quickly. He coughed up a fish and launched it at the latch on the truck's back hatch. The hatch flipped down and the scooter rode right up into the truck, and then launched the penguins onto the rooftops.

They zipped past a clothesline, and a towel wiped the octopus ink off of Skipper's face.

"I can see!" he cried, and the first thing he saw was Rico accidentally coughing up the green canister. "I can see! Rico, the glowing thing!"

Rico swallowed the canister again as a sock wrapped around Skipper's face.

"Agh! Venetian blinded again!" he yelled.

The gondola bounced off the rooftop and onto an awning, then bounced again onto the ground.

That's when an octopus jumped into the gondola with them.

"We've been boarded!" Kowalski yelled.

"Initiate self-destruct sequence!" Skipper ordered.

At that moment, a motorcycle burst out of an

alley and drove right through the gondola, breaking it in half! The penguins flew out of the gondola along with the guitar. They landed on the guitar and rode it like a surfboard down the sidewalk.

"Nice," Skipper told Kowalski. "Frankly, I'm surprised we had a self-destruct sequence."

Bam! The guitar crashed into a wall. The penguins tumbled off, dazed from the crash. As they staggered around, Skipper addressed them—still with the sock over his head.

"All right, boys, battle stance!" he said, his voice full of exhaustion.

"We're in battle stance, sir," Kowalski informed him as Rico yanked the sock off of Skipper's head.

"Oh, good!" Skipper said. He turned to face the three octopi approaching menacingly. "Now we, uh, spring our trap!"

Kowalski looked behind them. They had their backs against the wall.

"I'm not sure they're the ones who are trapped, sir," he said.

"Kowalski, remember our little talk about true

35

but unhelpful comments?" Skipper asked.

Kowalski nodded. "Yes, sir."

"Sometimes we just have to wing it!" Skipper said, ready to launch into a defense.

But before the penguins could make a move, a snowy owl with white feathers swooped down and carried off an octopus.

Kowalski watched in awe. "Wow!"

A baby seal popped out of a light fixture on the wall.

Boom! He took out the second octopus with a flash grenade.

Then a huge polar bear emerged from a telephone booth.

Zap! He hit the last octopus with a Taser.

The penguins watched, amazed, as the owl flew back down and the three animals lined up before them.

"Sorry for underestimating the plan, Skipper," Kowalski said.

"It's okay, Kowalski. Just don't ever doubt me again," Skipper said. Then he looked at the animals. "Now, what the heck is going on?"

His voice was drowned out by the scream of a jet as it soared above them. A large wolf rappelled off the craft and landed in front of them.

"Remain calm, penguins," he said, in a super-official voice. "You are now under the protection of the North Wind. You are welcome."

CHAPTER 6
The North Wind

The wolf flashed a badge with the letters NW engraved on it. The penguins looked at one another. North Wind? What was going on here?

There was no time to ask questions as the wolf, the owl, the polar bear, and the baby seal led them up to the jet, which hovered miraculously over the city. The craft had the letters VTOL painted on the side. They stood for Vertical Takeoff and Landing ship.

Once they got inside, the big polar bear eyed them. "Oh my gosh! You guys are sooo cute! Cute, so cute! You're so cute!" he cooed. He picked them all up in both arms and squeezed them in a bear hug. "Ooh! And cuddly, too!"

"Hey! Get away! No more hugs!" Skipper complained, trying to bat him away.

"It's like being licked by a basketful of puppy dogs!" the polar bear said happily.

"Corporal!" the wolf barked. The unit leader was steering the plane.

Corporal reluctantly put down the penguins.

"Chart a course back to North Wind headquarters," the wolf instructed him.

Corporal backed away, forming a heart with his hands and grinning at the penguins before getting back into mission mode.

Then the wolf nodded to the white snowy owl. "Eva, inform them that we're bringing in witnesses," he ordered.

Skipper didn't like the sound of that at all. "Private, Dibble me," he said.

Private handed him a bag of Cheezy Dibbles, and Skipper jumped onto the plane's dashboard.

"We're not going anywhere with you," he told

the wolf commander, stuffing a Dibble into his beak. "We don't even know who the heck you are!"

"The North Wind is an elite—" the commander began.

Crunch! Skipper chomped down on a Dibble.

"An elite undercover, interspecies—"

Crunch! Skipper chomped down again.

"Task—"

Crunch!

"Force, dedicated to helping—"

Crunch!

"Animals who can't help—"

Crunch!

"Themselves—"

Crunch!

"Like penguins," the wolf finished.

"Really?" asked Skipper, insulted. "And *you* are?"

"My name is classified," the wolf responded.

"Classified, eh? What is that, Dutch?" Skipper asked. "Can't really hear the accent."

"My name isn't 'Classified.' My name is classified because I am the team leader," he informed Skipper.

He swung around on his chair to face the rest of his team.

"The seal is Short Fuse, explosives expert," he said. "The bear is Corporal—he's our muscle. And the lovely lady in white is Eva, intelligence and analysis. We're an elite unit."

"Well, Agent Classified, we happen to be an elite unit too," Skipper said. For effect, he pressed one of the buttons on the dashboard with his foot.

"Self-destruct sequence activated in three . . . two . . . one . . . ," the computer calmly warned.

"You know, you should really label these things," Skipper said.

Classified pressed a button to end the self-destruct sequence.

"The name's Skipper," Skipper said. "I run this outfit. Back there is Kowalski. He's the brains of our operation. Say something smart, Kowalski."

But Kowalski was staring at Eva, his mouth wide open. He had never seen such a beautiful bird!

"See? He's working on a whole 'nother level," Skipper bragged. "And Rico, he's our demolition expert."

Rico hopped up onto Short Fuse's seat, jammed his head into the cushion, and popped up with the chair's stuffing in his mouth.

"He destroyed that chair for the sheer fun of it," Skipper said. "No reason at all! And then there's Private."

Private puffed out his chest and saluted.

"He's uh, sort of our secretary-slash-mascot," Skipper said.

Private tried to hide his disappointment. Is that all he was to the team?

"Cute," said Agent Classified, noticing his sad face.

"And cuddly," Corporal added.

Classified shot him a look.

"Sorry," Corporal said, and turned back to his computer screen.

The VTOL had swiftly cleared the continent and now soared over the icy northern Atlantic. Classified cranked the throttle forward, launching the craft into a steep dive, aiming at an iceberg floating on the water below.

"Let's see how cute and cuddly handles this next bit," Classified said under his breath.

But the penguins kept their cool as the VTOL zoomed toward the iceberg, looking like it was going to crash into it at any moment. Just before they made contact, a door slid open on the side of the iceberg, allowing them to fly inside.

"Nice doggy door," Skipper scoffed.

Classified brought the VTOL to a stop on a landing pad. Another door opened in front of them to reveal the North Wind headquarters: a massive high-tech fortress with dozens of agents scurrying about.

An announcement rang through the compound. *"Arrival. Pad seventeen. Arrival. Pad seventeen."*

The penguins peered out of the window, impressed.

"Well, well, well," said Skipper. "Not a bad place you got here, Classified."

"Thank you. That's not my name," the agent replied.

CHAPTER 7
Dave's Evil Plan

Moments later, the four penguins and the North Wind agents sat around a large table in the North Wind situation room. They faced a giant projection of a world map.

Classified stirred a cappuccino as he began the briefing. "All right, tiny penguins, the best way for the North Wind to protect helpless animals like yourselves is to bring Dr. Brine to justice. Now you were inside his sub, so I need to know everything you know."

He turned to the penguins to the answer, but they were too busy playing with their fancy hydraulic chairs. Skipper pressed a pedal and the chair shot up high. The others did the same.

"Yee-hoo!" Skipper cheered.

"Raaaah!" Rico growled.

"Haaaa!" cried Kowalski.

"Weeeee!" squealed Private.

Agent Classified was not amused. "Just tell me everything you know," he said, pulling out a notebook.

The penguins lowered their chairs and got serious—well, sort of.

"All right," Skipper began. "Hot dogs are in fact only seventeen percent actual dog."

Classified sighed. "Not *everything* everything. Just everything regarding your abduction by Dr. Octavius Brine."

He wheeled Skipper over to a photo of Dr. Brine on the evidence wall.

"Ah, why didn't you say so?" Skipper asked. "My team has uncovered that Dr. Octavius Brine is actually an individual known as Derek—"

"Dave," Kowalski corrected him.

"—as Dave the octopus," Skipper finished.

"An octopus?" Short Fuse laughed smugly. "No, Dr. Brine is not an octopus. He's—"

"An octopus! Precisely!" said Classified. "That's exactly what our intel indicated."

He coughed, and removed a photo of a sheep from the evidence wall. His guess had been way off, but he didn't want the penguins to know that.

Then he whispered into his watch. "Release the sheep."

He turned back to the penguins. "But what you of course, could *not* know, is that Dr. Brine's laboratory in Venice is secretly developing a doomsday weapon called the Medusa Serum."

Classified pointed to a picture of a canister filled with green goop.

"Ah, but what you don't know is that Dirk—" Skipper began.

"Dave," Kowalski corrected.

"Dave won't be using his Bazooka Serum—"

"Medusa Serum," said Kowalski.

"Medusa Serum on anybody!" finished Skipper.

Kowalski nodded. "That part is accurate."

"Show 'em, Rico!" Skipper ordered.

Rico coughed up the canister.

Classified looked stunned. "You . . . you stole the Medusa Serum?"

Skipper grinned triumphantly. "Well, 'stole the serum,' 'saved the day,' 'did your job for you,' call it what you will."

Classified growled just as a static sound filled the room. Suddenly, Dave's face appeared on the large screen!

"Debbie!" Skipper cried.

"Dave," Kowalski corrected him.

"Dave!" Skipper cried.

"He hacked into our system!" Corporal reported.

On the screen, Dave looked like he was giving an amazing, villainous speech, but there was no sound to go with it.

"Where's the sound?" Eva asked in a Russian accent. "I can't hear anything."

Kowalski yelled at the screen. "Dave! Your microphone. It's not on!"

Confused, Dave started pressing buttons.

"Click on the button with the picture of the microphone," Classified instructed.

Short Fuse frowned. "Every time a villain calls in, this happens. That's so annoying. Every time!"

Dave's screen froze and then went blank.

"Hello? Hello?" Dave's voice rang out.

"Now we can hear you, but we can't see you," Kowalski reported.

"I thought it was this button," Dave said, reaching again.

Classified sighed. "It's like talking to my parents."

The screen popped up again, and now they could see Dave wearing glasses and peering at buttons, his face close to the camera.

"How about now?" Dave asked.

The penguins and agents let out a cheer.

"Excellent. Now where was I?" Dave tossed his glasses, leaned in, and laughed evilly.

"Dave!" Kowalski cried.

"Greetings, North Wind," Dave began. "I see you've met my old zoo mates."

"We were never 'mates,'" Skipper corrected him.

"Turn yourself in, David," Agent Classified urged. "You're powerless now that I have your precious Medusa Serum."

He held up the canister for Dave to see.

"What? You! You didn't steal that!" Skipper protested.

"It's over," Agent Classified said, ignoring Skipper.

"It's over? Then why did I call you?" Dave asked. "Weird. Oh! Maybe it was to show you this."

Dave panned the camera to reveal a giant vat of the green serum behind him. Classified looked down at the small canister he was holding. Dave had much, much more.

"That's a lot of serum for four penguins," Kowalski noticed.

"Aw, you thought this was just for you four?" Dave asked. "No, no, no. We're just getting started. Now if you'll excuse me, I have to go do some shopping . . . for revenge!"

He fumbled with the buttons again. "Wait, how do you . . ."

His octopus henchmen helped him, and the screen finally flipped off.

Boop! Boop! A message flashed on the screen in front of Eva.

"Incoming alert!" she cried.

"Put it on the screen!" Classified commanded.

Eva typed on her keyboard, and the map of the world appeared back on the screen. A window popped up on the map with a picture of a penguin inside it.

"Berlin! Fifteen penguins missing," Eva reported.

"Dave's kidnapping other penguins!" Private cried.

"No doubt cute and cuddly," added Corporal.

"We have to move!" Agent Classified and Skipper said at the same time.

Then they looked at each other.

"What?" they both asked. They were both used to being the one in charge.

"Time for our 'A' game," Classified told his agents.

"Everybody huddle up!" Skipper told his team.

"Corporal, ready the jet," Classified said. "I'm

initiating North Wind Protocol Zeta."

Boop! Boop! Eva got another alert. "Twelve more penguins taken from London!" she informed them.

Skipper and the boys jumped into a huddle. "Okay, boys, this is it, the mission we've been preparing for our entire lives. We're gonna take down Dave or die trying."

He turned to Kowalski. "Cancel our improv class."

"Yes, sir!" Kowalski replied.

"Rico, equipify!" Skipper commanded.

Rico grunted.

"Private, do that little thing I like," Skipper ordered.

Private grinned and gave a silly salute.

"Ha-ha! It's still funny," Skipper said.

Kowalski put down his phone. "Skipper! Good news! I got them to credit our class."

The two teams sprang into action. While Corporal readied the VTOL, the penguins helped themselves to some cool gear. They raced back into the situation room loaded with rocket launchers, jet packs, and grenades.

"Aw yeah, baby!" Skipper cheered.

"They're stealing my stuff!" Short Fuse said angrily.

Agent Classified stepped in front of them.

"No! This mission is no place for a pathetic waddle of useless penguins!" he said firmly.

"Whoa! Whoa! Whoa! Who are you calling pathetic?" Skipper asked.

"Enough!" Classified shouted, pounding his paw on the table.

Rico was sitting right there. The table bumped up, he burped, and a rocket shot out of his mouth.

Boom! It crashed through the window and blew up the VTOL that Corporal had just prepared.

"See, Rico, that's why you can't have nice things," Skipper said.

Fwip! Agent Classified shot a tranquilizer dart at Skipper.

Instantly, Skipper's whole world went dark.

CHAPTER 8
Free Falling

Moments later, Agent Classified tucked all four penguins into a shipping box.

"Put on your jammies, penguins," Short Fuse said.

"They are even cute when they're asleep," Eva remarked, and Corporal nodded in agreement.

Short Fuse disagreed. "Not to me!"

"I want these butterballs out of my way, and out of my mission," Classified said. "Ship them to one of our safe houses. The most remote place on the planet—Madagascar."

The penguins didn't wake up until hours later.

They groaned groggily as they tried to figure out what happened.

"Ugh. Where the heck are we?" Skipper asked.

"Oxygen content is low," Kowalski said. "I suggest we limit our breathing."

Then the sound of a fart broke the silence.

"Aw, Private!" Skipper scolded.

Three beaks jammed through the cardboard of the shipping box. Private poked his beak out last.

"Sorry, I get gassy when I fly."

"He does!" Skipper remembered.

"We must be on a plane!" guessed Kowalski.

Wham! They burst out of the box and spilled out onto the floor.

"What did North Wind do to us?" Kowalski wondered.

"Oh! They gave us badges!" Private said. He pointed to a circular tag stuck to his skin.

"Not badges, tranquilizer darts!" Skipper said. He, Kowalski, and Rico plucked them out, but Private left his in. He liked it. It felt like a badge to him—and that made him feel important.

"Classified! That low-down dirty dog is trying to kick us off the mission!" Skipper fumed.

"He thinks we can't save the penguins because we're just . . . penguins," Kowalski said.

"Well, penguins are our flesh and feathers," said Skipper. "They're us! And if anyone is going to save us, it's us!"

"But, Skipper, we've gotta be five miles up," Kowalski pointed out. "That pretty much limits our options."

Skipper's eyes narrowed with determination. "I make my own options."

He slammed the cargo door release button with his flipper.

Whoosh! The door opened, sucking them out of the plane and into the air! A bunch of shipping packages flew out behind them.

"Aaaaaagh!" they screamed as they fell.

"Brilliant move, Skipper," Kowalski said, "but now we seem to be outside the plane."

"I kinda got caught up in the moment," Skipper admitted. "Okay, Kowalski, your turn to pick up the slack."

"Uh. . . ." Kowalski was out of ideas.

"Why don't we catch that plane?" Private asked, pointing to a jumbo jet sailing right toward them.

"Aaaaaaagh!" they screamed.

Slam! They smacked into its windshield. The pilot simply turned on the windshield wipers and swatted them off.

Knocked free, they hurtled toward more planes passing below.

"We've got another target, straight ahead at twelve o'clock," Kowalski said, using a military term to describe the location of target to where it would appear on a clock.

"Good, it's only eleven thirty," said Skipper. "Follow me, boys, we're going in hot!"

As they fell at superspeed, Private actually started to burst into flames!

"No one likes a show-off, Private," Skipper scolded.

"Aim for first class!" Kowalski yelled.

Smash! They tore through the plane's roof.

Chaos erupted as the passengers noticed them.

Private quickly jumped into an ice bucket, putting out his flames.

"Kowalski, where does this aircraft go?" Skipper asked.

Kowalski picked up a croissant from the nearest tray table. "From the odd shape of this bagel, I'd say we're headed for Paris."

"France? Forget it," Skipper declared.

"Then I would suggest a midair transfer," Kowalski said.

Skipper nodded. "Affirmative!"

Private walked by, pushing the plane's beverage cart.

"Peanuts, peanuts, peanuts!" he called out.

Skipper, Kowalski, and Rico hopped onto the cart and Private pushed it toward the cockpit. As they entered, the cart got caught on a chair, launching Skipper right onto the dashboard of the plane. He peered out of the cockpit window.

"There's our next ride, boys," he said, pointing toward a plane.

He hopped back onto the cart, and they rolled

backward down the aisle. The penguins burst through the emergency exit and began to free fall once more.

"Deploy flaps!" Kowalski yelled.

The cart's side panels folded out like a makeshift pair of wings as they tried to steer toward the next plane.

"Stay on target!" cried Skipper.

"We're going to catch it! We're going to catch it!" Private shouted as they zoomed toward the jet.

Whoosh! The flaps ripped off, and they lost their ability to steer. They flew right past the jet.

"Crikey!" exclaimed Private. "We're not going to catch it!"

Kowalski looked around. "Wait a minute. Where's Skipper?"

Rico pointed above them. They looked to see Skipper standing on one of the boxes that had ejected from the first plane. A trail of boxes followed behind him, caught in the air current.

"Time to get creative!" Skipper called down. "Start grabbing boxes, boys!"

Rico picked up Private and tossed him like a football at one of the boxes.

"Going long! Hoo-hoo!" Private cheered as he sailed through the air. He crashed into a box, sending packing peanuts flying out. When he popped back up, he had a parachute strapped to his back!

"Aw, Private, stop playing with those backpacks," Skipper said. "Find something useful!"

Rico jumped into a box and searched through it. Then he began to murmur with excitement. He pointed to a tube jutting out of the box.

"Now we're talking," said Skipper. "Let's get to work!"

Skipper and Kowalski jumped into the box with Rico. They started to pump his feet as he blew air into the tube. But the cargo in the box wasn't inflating fast enough.

Anxious, Kowalski looked at the ground, which was quickly approaching below them. "Four hundred meters . . . three hundred meters . . ."

"Speak American, Kowalski!" Skipper snapped.

"Sorry, sir," Kowalski said. "Two hundred eighteen

59

yards . . . one hundred nine yards . . . "

Rico gave one final, massive puff, and a fully inflated, jungle-themed bounce house burst from the box. It landed softly on the ground, and the four penguins happily bounced on top of it.

"Okay, then," said Skipper. "It's clear what we need to do next."

One hour later . . . they were still giddily bouncing up and down. Finally, they slid off.

"Impressive bouncing, boys," Skipper said. "Now, then, back to civilization. If we're gonna take Dexter down, we need to know where he is going to strike. But first, who needs to take a whiz?"

CHAPTER 9
One Step Behind

The North Wind agents were one step ahead of the penguins—but one step behind Dave. Under the cover of night, they investigated the penguin habitat at a zoo in Brazil. They flew overhead in a new VTOL, taking rapid photos using heat technology.

The photos projected up inside the plane.

Eva analyzed them. "Penguin footprints are still warm."

"Blast it! He's gone!" Classified said.

"Blast it! He's gone! Shoot!" echoed Short Fuse.

A map of the zoos with missing penguins

appeared on the screen. The map of the zoo in Brazil lit up to join them.

Short Fuse was hopping mad. "Boy, if I ever needed some penguins kidnapped, I know who I'm calling! Look at this map. Dave took your penguins! Tokyo, London, Paris, Rio. Amsterdam? Amster-*BAM*!"

Corporal growled, frustrated. "So . . . many . . . penguins!"

He ripped out the computer keyboard and shoved it in his mouth, chewing on it.

"Corporal. CORPORAL!" Classified scolded, trying to pull the keyboard away from him. Eva and Short Fuse tried to calm him down by stroking his fur.

"There, there," said Eva.

"Rub the angry out of the tummy," Short Fuse said. "There it goes. Bye-bye, angry."

"Corporal! Listen to me!" Classified said firmly. "Focus on the sound of my voice. My rich, sooth-ing voice. Yes, we are going to save those helpless penguins because we are the North Wind, and no one . . . *no one* breaks the Wind!"

The words gave Corporal courage. He opened his mouth and let the keyboard drop to the floor.

"No one breaks the Wind," he repeated.

"There's a good Corporal," Classified said. "We rescued four penguins already, didn't we? Shipped them off all cozy and snug to a Madagascar safe hou—how come there's beeping?"

Boop! Boop!

Eva checked her screen. "Sir, about those penguins. They never made it to Madagascar."

Classified couldn't believe it. "What? Where are they?"

On the other side of the world, a manhole cover opened on a busy city street. The four penguins emerged into a colorful scene. Merchants sold vegetables, fish, and exotic fabrics from market stalls. Signs written in Chinese characters announced goods and sales. People whizzed by on bicycles and scooters.

"Kowalski, what are our coordinates?" Skipper asked.

"From my calculations, we've arrived in Dublin, Ireland," he replied.

But they were far from Ireland. They had actually arrived in Shanghai, the largest city in China.

"All right, soldiers. We gotta blend in," Skipper said. "Everyone, quick—do an Irish jig!"

The penguins danced out of the manhole and popped up inside a street stall selling dolls.

"No time for sightseeing boys," Skipper began. "We need to find intel on Dave's location, pronto!"

Then he spotted something. "Aha!"

He hopped over to a market stall selling baby squid on ice. He grabbed one and slapped it.

"All right, you! Where's Dave? Give us the goods!"

Kowalski coughed. "Sir, that's a baby squid."

"Waaa!" wailed the baby squid.

"Sorry, laddie." Skipper placed the baby squid back down and began to pace in front of his men.

"Ugh. Stranded on the Emerald Isle, without a single clue!" Skipper said. "Well, so much for the luck of the Irish."

Kowalski pointed. "Skipper, look!"

Behind Skipper, a large TV screen on one of the buildings was blaring a story about the missing penguins. The newscaster was speaking in Mandarin, but they got the idea. A world map popped up, showing the locations of all the disappearances.

"It looks like Dave's been busy," Kowalski said. "He's stolen penguins from Guadalajara, Mexico!"

"Madrid, Spain!" said Private.

"Parie!" said Skipper.

"Athens, Greece!" added Kowalski.

Rico got a thoughtful look on his face. He began to cough up the snow globes he had swallowed in Dave's hideout.

The penguins keep counting off the cities with missing penguins. Bangalore, Düsseldorf, Osaka, Rio de Janeiro, Nairobi, Amsterdam, Baton Rouge. . . .

Skipper, Kowalski, and Private looked back to see the snow globe collection piled next to Rico.

"Dave's snow globe collection . . ." Skipper realized.

"It's every zoo and aquarium he got kicked out of!" Kowalski finished.

Skipper looked at Rico. "Don't tell me where he *has* been. Tell me where he *will* have been next."

Rico began to cough up something else, but it got caught in his throat.

"Wait, what is it, Rico?" Skipper asked.

Bwaack! Rico choked.

"It's a book! It's a film! It's a play!" Skipper guessed.

Bwaack! Rico just couldn't cough it up.

"First word . . . ," Skipper said.

Bwaack!

"Two syllables," Skipper said. "Sounds like *bwaak*? What starts with *bwaack*?"

Rico's belly rumbled as he coughed up one last globe. An emblem on the front read SHANGHAI.

"Shanghai," Skipper said thoughtfully.

Kowalski pointed to the world map on the TV screen—there was no symbol on Shanghai.

"Dave hasn't been there yet, Skipper!" Kowalski figured out. "If we hurry, we can still stop him!"

"Nice work, Rico," Skipper said. "Pack your bags, boys! It's time to blow this potato stand."

The boys quickly packaged themselves in a box labeled SHANGHAI and tossed themselves onto a delivery truck. The truck took off—and then doubled back. A worker chucked the box out of the van.

They were in the exact same spot as before—but they thought they had traveled far.

"Skipper, look!" Private said, pointing to a poster plastered to a nearby building. It read MERMAID PENGUINS AT SHANGHAI MARINE WORLD AQUARIUM and there was a logo for an aquarium in Shanghai.

"I see you, Private," Skipper said, chuckling. "Who's a big boy standing on his toes?"

"What? No, I mean the—" Private began, but Skipper wouldn't let him finish.

"I just wanna eat you up," he said, pinching Private's cheek.

"Skipper, look! Above Private!" Kowalski cried.

They all looked at the poster that Private had been trying to point out.

"Good eye, Kowalski," Skipper praised him. "And once again, you have proven that you're a meaningful and valued member of the team."

Kowalski beamed, but Private sighed.

He didn't mind being cute. But he was more than just a cute and cuddly penguin. When would Skipper ever realize that he was a meaningful and valued member of the team too?

CHAPTER 10
See the Penguin Mermaids!

While the penguins made their way to the Shanghai aquarium, Dave's sub glided through the water, headed for China. Inside, dozens of octopi henchmen were busy carrying cages of stolen penguins through the sub's twisted hallways.

Dressed as Octavius Brine, Dave wiggled through the hallways, talking to the penguins. "Welcome aboard! Joaquin, Ignacio, Jordan . . . you are all just adorable!" he said.

Then he turned to his henchmen. "Anthony and Michael—haul them away!"

He stormed off to the submarine's bridge, where

one of his men, Nicholas, was marking off cities on a world map while other octopus henchmen scurried about busily. "Outstanding," said Dave. "We're on a roll, gentlemen. Now where are we on tracking down Skipper and his boys?"

Nicholas drew a circle around the entire world and shrugged. He had no idea.

"Well then, you'd better start looking," Dave said, unusually cheerful.

Still smiling, he grabbed Nicholas and hit a button on his chair. A panel popped open on the nearest wall, revealing an open torpedo tube. Dave hurled Nicholas into the tube and then pressed another button on his chair marked fire.

Whoosh! Nicholas launched into the murky water. Dave turned to his henchmen as the sub began to surface.

"Find me those penguins, and let's keep this revenge train hummin'!" Dave said with evil glee. "Chugga, chugga, choo! Chugga, chugga, choo! Woo-woo!"

Then he plopped into his chair as the sub broke

through the water. In front of him rose a skyline of tall buildings, huge pagodas, and colorful neon signs.

"Bring her up, boys," he said. "Give me the postcard view. Next stop, Shanghai!"

"Ladies and gentlemen, we are pleased to present . . . the world famous mermaid penguins!" introduced the announcer at the Shanghai aquarium. On a stage above a large tank, several big, fake clamshells opened up. Inside were adorable penguins fitted with mermaid costumes—bathing suit tops and long, shimmery fish tails. They dove into the water and began to perform for the crowd.

"Penguin feeding time will be in two minutes," said the announcer.

Meanwhile, Skipper and his crew had stationed themselves around the aquarium, ready to jump into action at any sign of Dave or his crew.

The four penguins were in the jaws of a shark model hanging from the ceiling. They watched the action below with binoculars.

"All right, fellas. Keep your eyes open," Skipper instructed. "Dave's a master of disguise. He could be anywhere. You're up, Private." He nudged the souvenir mermaid backpack next to him.

"Do I have to?" Private asked.

"Out, out, out," Skipper ordered.

The backpack unzipped, and Private stepped out, wearing a full mermaid costume.

Skipper gasped with delight. "You just mer-made my day!"

"But I don't want to be a diversion," Private told Skipper. "That's a job for someone who's cute but otherwise useless."

Skipper didn't notice a word he was saying. "I've got your back, Private. Have I ever let you down before?"

"No, Skipper," Private said.

"That's the spirit!" Skipper cheered. "Deploy!"

Skipper shoved Private. He spun to a stop in front of the tank, right between Dave and the crowd.

"Look, they let one of the mermaids out of the tank!" a little boy cried.

"He's so cute!" squealed a little girl.

"Awww!" The crowd sighed as they surrounded Private. He gave Skipper a final disappointed look before turning to face them.

Skipper suddenly was decked out like a super-spy. He peered through a pair of binoculars and spotted Dave in his awkward Dr. Brine human disguise. Dr. Brine wore an old-fashioned diving suit with a mask and carried a bucket of fish.

Rico burst out of the janitor's closet, riding a vacuum cleaner and wielding a plunger. He shoved the plunger into the vacuum and perched on the long handle like a witch riding a broom. Then he flipped the vacuum into reverse.

The vacuum shot out the plunger, sending Rico flying across the room. He soared behind Dave's back and the plunger hit a glass tank.

Turning, Rico saw that he had attached the plunger to his target: a tank holding three angry leopard seals. They rammed into the glass, trying to get to Rico. *Wham! Wham! Wham!*

Back in the whale room, Kowalski furiously sawed

at the wires holding up the whale skeleton. He didn't notice that nearby, a laser-cut circle appeared on the ceiling. The four North Wind agents dropped down to the floor.

"Those fools are here somewhere," Agent Classified guessed.

Splash! The seals shattered the glass of their tank and spilled out, sliding across the hall in a rush of water.

So far, the plan was working perfectly!

The flood swept Dave out of the hall and right into the whale room. The North Wind agents dodged the water just in time.

Over at the mermaid tank, the tourists had no clue what was happening behind them. An aquarium employee noticed the fuss over Private and picked him up.

"What are you doing out here, cutie?" she asked. "Come on, back in your tank."

In the whale room, a confused and groggy Dave staggered to his feet. His tentacles dangled out of his disheveled diving suit.

"Dave!" Agent Classified yelled.

Crash! The whale skeleton came down right on time, trapping Dave in a bony jail cell.

Kowalski leaped down from the ceiling. Skipper and Rico belly-slid into the room.

"Little late, North Wind," Kowalski said triumphantly.

Skipper gave a little bow. "You're welcome!"

"Corporal, take our prisoner into custody," Classified ordered.

"You mean *our* prisoner," Skipper said.

"He belongs to us!" challenged Classified.

"He's ours! We caught him!" Skipper shot back.

"You will stand down and leave this to the professionals!" Classified commanded loudly.

Corporal pried open the whale's rib cage—revealing Dave's diving suit crumpled on the floor.

"Dave's not here," Corporal remarked.

Skipper and Classified both turned to look. "What?"

"You melted him?" Short Fuse asked. "You birds are sick!"

Kowalski stepped into the cage and moved the diving suit aside, revealing a drain underneath. His face fell as he realized the truth.

"He's going in through the pipes!"

Skipper, Kowalski, Rico, and the North Wind raced toward the tank holding the mermaid penguins. But Dave got there first. He popped open the drain and reached up with his tentacles, grabbing the mermaid penguins and dragging them down with him one by one.

By the time Skipper, Kowalski, and Rico got to the tank, they could see Private being dragged into the drain.

"No, no, no!" Skipper yelled.

"Skipper! Heeelp!" Private gurgled. Then he was dragged down the pipe and disappeared down the drain.

"Private! No! What have I done?" Skipper wailed.

Rico grabbed a metal post holding up the line ropes and smashed it into the tank. The penguins leaped inside and dove down the drain after their brother.

CHAPTER 11
The Chase

Skipper, Kowalski, and Rico swam through the pipe, which led to the ocean waters. Breaking the surface, they could see Dave's submarine speeding away.

"He's got Private! He's getting away! He's getting away! Rico, do something!" Skipper pleaded, frantic.

But Rico was frantic too. He nervously hiccupped a bunch of objects, but none of them were helpful.

"Kowalski, give me options! I need options!" Skipper begged.

"Options! Options! Options!" Kowalski couldn't

think straight. How could he, when Private was gone?

Then Skipper remembered something. "Activate Emotional Override protocol!"

"Yes, sir!" Kowalski replied.

He slapped Skipper. Skipper slapped Rico. Rico slapped Kowalski. Then they did it again.

Finally, they could think clearly.

Kowalski pointed to the VTOL at the end of the dock.

"Skipper, the North Wind's plane!"

Skipper's eyes lit up. "Sweet chariot of the gods! But can you fly it, man?"

"There's only one way to find out," Kowalski said, his voice more serious than ever.

A few minutes later, Kowalski was sprawled out on the floor of the VTOL with the owner's manual while Skipper and Rico impatiently tapped their feet.

"No, I still cannot read," Kowalski reported.

Skipper slapped the manual out of Kowalski's flippers.

"Then we're going off book!"

The North Wind rushed up to the pier just as the

VTOL jerkily flew up into the air. It spun wildly. A missile shot out and hit the water. The North Wind agents ducked.

"No, no, no, no, no!" Agent Classified roared.

Inside the VTOL, Kowalski sat in the pilot's seat, slapping a computer keyboard.

"I'm getting the hang of this, Skipper!" he said.

Actually, the VTOL was completely upside down. But that didn't matter to the penguins.

"Good! Now let's get our boy," Skipper said.

The jet blasted off, leaving the North Wind agents coughing on exhaust.

"Those ludicrous butterballs are letting David escape!" he fumed. "Eva, transport! Short Fuse, Corporal, hitch us a ride!"

Eva rocketed ahead. With her head, she rammed a small boat into position at the end of the dock.

Short Fuse whipped out a pen and clicked it. It transformed into a giant cable gun.

Corporal hoisted Short Fuse and the big gun onto his shoulder.

Bam! He fired. A long cable shot out. A magnetic

79

head on the end attached to the bottom of the VTOL.

Classified jumped into Eva's boat. Short Fuse jumped off Corporal and headed for the boat. Grabbing the cable, Corporal skied on the pier, landing in the boat. Now the VTOL towed the boat while Eva flew alongside it.

Then Classified hooked himself to a pulley, and he attached the pulley to the cable attached to the VTOL. He began to hoist himself up the cable toward the jet.

Inside the plane, Kowalski watched the blips on the radar screen showing the position of the VTOL and the position of Dave's sub.

"Sir, Dave is pulling ahead!" Kowalski cried. "We're too heavy!"

Skipper angrily looked down at his gut.

"Curse our heavily Cheezy-Dibbled diet! Rico, give me a fire sale!" he ordered.

Rico nodded happily.

"*Everything* must go!" Skipper told him.

Rico opened a hatch in the floor and started

chucking down every loose object in reach. Coffee cups, helmets, chairs—they all went flying out of the plane . . . and rained down on Agent Classified! He grunted as a stapler whacked him in the face.

"Not good. Ow!" he complained.

Within minutes, the four penguins and the control panel were all that was left in the VTOL.

"That's everything, sir," Kowalski reported.

"Have you purged the chemical toilet?" Skipper asked.

"But Rico was in there for fifteen minutes!" Kowalski protested.

"Just do it!" Skipper thundered.

Kowalski pulled a cord, ejecting the stinky blue toilet water from the plane. The penguins couldn't hear it, but outside the plane, Agent Classified let out a horrified wail. "Noooooooooooo!"

Classified landed back in the boat, streaked with blue. Corporal wrinkled his nose. "Ew!"

Short Fuse scooted across the boat. "I respect you, boss," he said. "I'm just gonna respect you from over here."

Frustrated, Classified grabbed the wheel of the boat and steered around a tall, jagged rock jutting out of the water. The cable attached to the VTOL and wound around the rock, stopping the plane in midair.

The sudden stop knocked the penguins off their feet. Rico's face hit the button marked self-destruct.

"Self-destruct activated in five . . . ," the computer began.

"No! Private!" Skipper cried. They *couldn't* self-destruct. They had to help their little buddy!

"Four . . . three . . ."

Skipper's heart was breaking as he watched the submarine sink beneath the water. "All alone in that cold, metal death sausage."

"Two . . ."

Kowalski scrambled to reach the eject button.

"Stay strong, soldier!" Skipper shouted down toward the water.

"One. . . ."

The three penguins ejected through the floor of the cockpit.

Eva quickly figured out what was going on. "Abandon ship!" she yelled.

Boom! The VTOL exploded above them. The North Wind agents dove out of their boat just as Skipper, Kowalski, and Rico crash-landed into it, tearing the boat to pieces.

CHAPTER 12
Adrift at Sea

The sun baked down on Skipper, Kowalski, and Rico as they floated on the ocean waves, clutching a piece of the broken boat.

"Skipper's log," Skipper began. "Private has been kidnapped by Dave, while we have been cast adrift for what seems like days. No rations, fresh water, or land in sight. Kowalski is sick as a dog, and Rico keeps trying to eat him."

Poor Kowalski was leaning over the side of the debris, seasick. Wild-eyed, Rico had firmly clamped his beak onto Kowalski's rear end.

"Please just cut it out!" Kowalski complained.

"Not sure how we can hold on," Skipper said, his voice weak. "This may be my final entry."

Pop! The cork from a bottle of sparkling nectar hit Skipper in the face.

He looked up to see the North Wind comfortably eating a meal in their inflatable emergency pod. That conceited crew had rescued the penguins, tying their busted-up boat to the North Wind pod in order to tow it. Their furry leader had said something about them blowing up too many planes. Preposterous!

In the pod, Short Fuse was pouring the bubbly drink for Agent Classified. The wolf sniffed it.

"Mmm. Hints of pear, white peaches," he said contentedly.

Eva dined off a china plate. "Mmm. This salmon is delicious."

"I've never been more hydrated in my life!" said Short Fuse, gulping down a glass of water.

Eva turned to Agent Classified. "Let me cut you a piece of this salmon. It's the most delicious thing on the boat."

"No, thank you, I'm stuffed," Classified replied. "Ugh. I'll have to loosen my utility belt."

Corporal held out a plate of herring to Short Fuse.

"No, I'm full," the baby seal replied. "Just dump it in the ocean."

The penguins watched helplessly as Corporal tossed the herring overboard.

Skipper scowled at Classified. "You know, we're all in the same boat here."

"Actually, we're not," Classified replied. "And perhaps you could express a little more concern over the fact that you've stolen and destroyed a ninety million dollar vehicle."

"Bill me," Skipper shot back.

Beep!

"Corporal?" Classified asked.

"We're picking up a signal, sir," Corporal reported, reading the radar screen. "It's five clicks southwest. But it's stopped at that remote island."

He pointed ahead, toward a small, crescent-shaped island.

Skipper paddled forward to get a better look.

"Land? Good on you! You've tracked down some land!" he said.

"No, silly Willy," said Short Fuse. "We've been tracking your little secretary-slash-mascot."

"What? You put a homing device on Private?" Skipper asked incredulously.

Classified held up his dart gun.

"All of you, actually, when I darted you," he replied smugly.

Skipper hopped into the pod and got in Classified's face.

"You low-down, dirty, mangy, filthy, flea-bitten toilet drinker," he told him, but he paused. That low-down, dirty, mangy, filthy, flea-bitten toilet drinker had found Private. "But . . . good."

"See? I told you. You should have left this to the professionals," Classified said. He bit down on a biscotti, and the crumbs flew into Skipper's face. Skipper didn't notice. He stared uneasily at the island.

Private was there, somewhere. But was he all right?

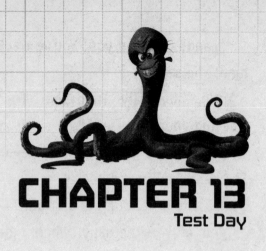

CHAPTER 13
Test Day

Private was inside Dave's submarine, trapped in a cage with the mermaid penguins from the aquarium. A pair of octopus henchmen wheeled the cage past dozens of other penguins in a long hall.

The other penguins had been caged for a long time now. One of them counted off the days with tally marks on the cage floor. Another played a harmonica, while another did push-up after push-up.

Dave entered the hall, leaping and swinging from cage to cage with his tentacles. He smiled at the penguins as he passed them.

"Penguins! Ahoy there!" he greeted them. "Peeeenguiiins . . ."

He jumped onto the cage with the mermaid penguins.

"I bet you're dying to know why I brought you here," he said.

One of the mermaid penguins cracked from the stress. "He's gonna kill us all!" she screamed.

"What? No. Ew," said Dave. "My Medusa Serum doesn't kill anyone. Where's the fun in that?"

Private was surprised to hear it. He wanted more information—but he didn't want to give up his disguise either.

Dave laughed and pretended he was a game-show host. "So what *does* it do, Dave?" he asked himself. "Let's find out!"

Dave pulled out a random cricket from the group. "Ready . . . ," he said.

"No. Not ready. I could use a minute, actually," the cricket protested.

Dave ignored the cricket's protests and gave him to one of his henchmen.

"Elijah, would you do the honors?" Dave said. "Goggles, everyone!"

The henchmen put on safety glasses just as the giant ray came to life. A series of lights blinked on, illuminating the serum within.

The penguins looked on nervously as Dave pressed a button on the remote.

Zap! The ray fired. A blast of green light electrified the room as a laser crackled loudly.

The cricket grew to a monstrous size. His cute little face transformed into a hideous mask.

Dave continued speaking like a game-show host. "And what comes next, Dave? INVASION! Horrible mutant penguins unleashed on the streets of New York City!" Dave then screamed like a panicked human.

"Crikey!" Private cried, horrified.

Dave's head turned at the sound of Private's voice. He quickly clamped his beak shut.

"Who said that?" Dave asked.

He rushed to the mermaid cage and pulled open the cage door. One by one, he tossed the mermaid penguins aside until he came to Private. Then he ripped off Private's costume.

"Yes!" Dave cheered. He grabbed Private and held him up "Gentlemen, you remember Private."

The henchmen waved.

"You'll never get away with this!" Private said furiously. "My brothers are coming, and they're gonna get you."

Dave grinned. "Call off the hunt, everyone," he told his henchmen. "Turns out, the 'elite unit' will be coming to us." Then he tapped Private's beak. "Boop!"

The sun set as the North Wind reached the island. They landed and then spread out to watch what was happening with Dave's submarine.

"Eva, what do you see?" Agent Classified asked over the radio.

Eva watched the sub through a pair of binoculars. "My count is thirty hostiles."

"Thirty-one," said a voice next to her.

Startled, Eva pulled back to see that Kowalski was

right next to her, looking through the other eyepiece.

Kowalski got flustered. "Uh, those two octopi are very close together. I mean, you know. . . ."

At that moment Rico rose up on the other side of Eva with a coconut on his head for camouflage. Skipper popped up by Kowalski, with a banana strapped to his head.

"Ix-nay on the irt-flay, Kowalski," Skipper warned. Then he sighed. "Poor Private. Alone. Helpless in the belly of that beast."

"We've faced some long odds before, Skipper," Kowalski said. "But these look like the longest . . . and the oddest. If we're gonna pull this off, we'll need a diversion. And fast."

Behind them, the green leafy jungle background started to blink and flash.

"*Deactivating jungle camouflage,*" a computer announced.

The holographic screen fizzled out, revealing Classified, Short Fuse, and Corporal.

"Shh! Will you be quiet?" Classified whispered to Skipper.

Skipper frowned. "Listen, Classified—"

Classified cut Skipper off by turning the hologram back on and disappearing behind it.

"Short Fuse, you were supposed to handcuff them to the raft!" he scolded the baby seal.

"Don't you hologram me!" Skipper shouted. He then walked over to the holoscreen controls and shut it off.

"I tried, but they don't have hands," Short Fuse explained to his commander. "They just have flippers, boss, and I have flippers, so it's flipping useless!"

Skipper marched up to Classified. "All right, if you won't work with us, you'd better work for us. Our plan requires a diversion."

"I give the orders around here, and as much as it pains me, I need you to act as a diversion for our operation. Understood?" Classified asked.

"No," Skipper replied. "This is *our* plan, and it requires *you* to cause a diversion."

Skipper and Classified got into each other's faces. Besides everything else they disagreed on, they couldn't agree on how to pronounce the word "diversion."

"Die-version," said Classified.

"Dih-version," countered Skipper.

"Die," said Classified.

"Dih," said Skipper.

"Die."

"Dih."

"Die."

"Dih."

"Die."

"Dih."

"Die!"

"Dih!"

"Die! Die!" yelled Classified, more frustrated than ever.

"Gentlemen, there's only one way to resolve this," Eva began.

Kowalski stared at her, totally smitten. "We should kiss!" he blurted out.

"A Plan-off!" said Eva at the same time.

Kowalski blushed. "Yep, a Plan-off, that's what

I was going to say," he said quickly. "A Plan-off."

The North Wind agents and penguins retreated to the beach for the Plan-off. Skipper and Classified would each present their plan—and the best plan would win!

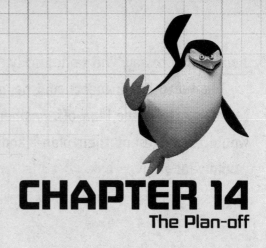

CHAPTER 14
The Plan-off

Skipper began the Plan-off by sketching a simple submarine shape in the sand.

"Here's Dave's sub," he said, and then moved a small rock inside the sub. "And this young, helpless, vulnerable rock is Private."

Kowalski and Rico waddled over with a pineapple made up to look like Octavius Brine.

"And here's Dave," Skipper said. "While you four dih-vert the octopi, we strike fast and strike hard."

He attacked the pineapple with punches and kicks.

"Heeeiiiiyeeeaah!" he cried. "Get on in here,

boys. Slap him silly, Rico, come on!"

Kowalski and Rico joined in.

"Kowalski, free the hostages!" Skipper yelled.

Corporal got into the spirit too. The polar bear smashed the pineapple with his big fist.

"Now that's what I'm talking about, big fella," Skipper praised him.

Classified glared at Corporal, who jumped back into position.

"With Private freshly liberated, we celebrate with a well-earned high-one and a feast of Dave's sweet remains. Any questions?" Skipper asked.

The penguins cheered and slapped flippers.

Classified clapped slowly.

"Wow, I mean, truly impressive," he said, his voice thick with sarcasm. "Especially the bit where you slap the fruit. Oh!"

He turned to his team. "Corporal, dim the lights. Short Fuse, glasses."

Corporal snuffed out their campfire while Short Fuse handed 3-D glasses to everyone. Classified dropped a cube onto the sand. It instantly transformed into a holographic 3-D dome that surrounded them with maps, charts, and graphs.

Kowalski was impressed. "Ooh!"

So was Rico. "Whoaa!"

Skipper, frowning, refused to be impressed.

Exciting music played, and the image of Dave's sub popped up on the dome.

"My apologies, had to rush a bit, the schematic's a little crude," Classified said. "At twenty-one fifty, Skipper, Kowalski, and Richard, is it?—will die-vert the octopi away from their posts."

The hologram showed octopi guarding the outside of the sub. They disappeared one by one as Classified explained his plan.

"At twenty-two hundred, Short Fuse breaches the hull with a swarm of self-guided underwater nanocharges," Classified went on as Kowalski and Rico watched, entranced.

In the hologram, an image of Short Fuse swam up to the sub and fired a burst of tiny pellets at it. They spiraled in and attached themselves to the sub's spinning propulsion system. One by one the pellets exploded, damaging the propulsion and creating an opening in the hull.

"I call them Wet Booms," Short Fuse said proudly.

"Yes, please don't," said Classified.

Short Fuse nodded. "Okay, sorry, sorry."

"At zero-nine-zero-two, knock-knock," Classified went on.

"Who's there?" asked Corporal.

"The North Wind," replied Classified.

"The North Wind, who?" Corporal asked.

"The North Wind who doesn't have time for knock-knock jokes because we're too busy taking down Dave," Classified said with a satisfied grin.

Skipper's eyes were glazing over. Sure, Classified's plan had a bunch of fancy stuff, but that didn't mean it was better than their pineapple plan, was it?

Classified gleefully went over their available equipment. "Personal hovertank? Check. Auto-targeting wing mounts? Why not? Oh, and what's this?"

Skipper tuned out completely as Classified blabbed on and on, explaining exactly how they were going to take down Dave and rescue the penguins.

"At twenty-two-zero-nine, mission accomplished!" Classified finished.

Boom! The submarine in the hologram exploded. An image of Agent Classified appeared, walking out of the wreckage unharmed and dragging Dave behind him.

"See that? I don't even look back," Classified bragged. "There's a huge explosion, and I just keep walking."

The hologram zipped back into the cube. There was a stunned silence as the North Wind broke into applause. Kowalski and Rico's minds were blown.

"Way to go, boss!" cheered Short Fuse. "That's North Wind, sucker!"

"Nicely done," added Corporal.

Skipper saw the doubt in Kowalski and Rico's eyes. He stepped forward.

"Well, la-di-da, blah blah blah," he said. "A good plan is about more than effecty stuff and vocabulary words."

"Oh, and you, you certainly know a good plan," said Classified, sarcastically again. "I mean, your operation in Shanghai allowed Dave to escape with your boy."

His words felt like a punch in the gut to Skipper.

"I've never lost a member of my team," Classified went on. "It must feel awful. Can't imagine the guilt, the regret. The feeling that, I don't know, it should have been you."

Skipper's heart broke at that moment. He looked down at the sand, at his sketch of the sub with the poor little rock representing Private trapped inside. He had a mental image of Private, who smiled up at him, so trusting.

"All for penguin plan?" Eva asked.

Loyal to the end, Kowalski and Rico raised their flippers.

"All for North Wind plan?" Eva asked.

Classified's team raised a wing, a flipper, and a paw—and Skipper raised his flipper too!

"His," Skipper said, beaten. "His is better."

"What?" Kowalski asked, and Rico looked upset.

"Sorry, boys, but I can't lead you this time," Skipper said.

"But . . . we're a team," Kowalski said. "And you're our skipper, Skipper. We don't need these guys."

Skipper shook his head. "No, Kowalski. But Private does. I think this time we leave it to the professionals."

"But, sir—" Kowalski protested.

Skipper held up a flipper to stop him. "It's settled. We take orders from Agent Classified now."

Rico's eyes teared up.

"That's an order, Rico," Skipper said.

He turned away to hide his true feelings. Skipper was devastated. He hated to turn things over to Agent Classified. But in his heart, he felt like it was the best thing to do for Private. He took a deep breath and turned to face his fluffy new commander.

"All right, Classified. What's the diversion?" Skipper asked.

Classified grinned. Wait till the penguins found out what was in store. . . .

CHAPTER 15
Sub Attack!

Later that night, Skipper, Kowalski, and Rico waddled up to the octopi guarding the sub. The penguins were wearing lederhosen, short pants with suspenders. Skipper held an accordion. All three of them smiled goofily.

They lined up, just as they had been instructed.

Skipper was mortified. "We never tell a soul we did this. We take this shame to our graves," Skipper told his crew, through a clenched beak.

"Agreed," said Kowalski.

Then Skipper started playing the accordion, and the three penguins launched into a German folk dance. The octopi stared curiously at the penguins at first. Then they started clapping to the music. Kowalski and Rico slapped each other's flippers as part of the dance, and the henchmen copied them.

The penguins danced their way down the dock, away from the submarine and into the surrounding jungle. Transfixed by the music and dancing, the henchmen followed them.

Below the pier, the North Wind agents waited for the guards to clear out.

"Time?" Classified asked Eva.

"Twenty-two hundred hours," she replied.

Classified nodded. "Time to take down Dave."

The agents burst out of hiding, dressed in all their high-tech gear. They entered the sub, using electrical charges and lasers to burst through door after door. Corporal gave a big polar bear punch to any guard that stood in their way.

The four North Wind agents stopped in front of Dave's captain's chair and trained their weapons on him.

"Dave the octopus!" Agent Classified shouted. "Show me your tentacles!"

Dave casually swung around in his chair and raised his tentacles.

"All of them," Classified ordered.

Slam! Dozens of octopus henchmen dropped from above, smashing the North Wind agents underneath them.

Back in the jungle, the octopus guards frantically searched for the adorable penguin folk dancers. Where had they gone?

After they disappeared into the forest, Skipper, Kowalski, and Rico dropped down from a tree branch, sitting on the accordion.

"We lost them, Skipper," Kowalski noted.

"And not a moment too soon," Skipper said, hoisting up his lederhosen. "These hosen are riding up in my Bundesliga."

They hopped down from the accordion. Kowalski picked up Rico and planted him upside down in the dirt. Then he studied the shadow Rico cast under the moonlight.

"Classified should be walking away from a huge

explosion with Private on his shoulder in three . . . two. . . . Give him a welcome home, Rico!" Skipper said.

Rico leaned his head back and hocked up fireworks that exploded in the air above them. But there was no sign of Private or the North Wind.

"Um, the sub didn't explode. I fear the fireworks may have been a tactical mistake," Kowalski said.

Wham! A horde of octopus henchmen dropped down upon the penguins.

By the time the penguins realized what was happening, they found themselves in a cage being wheeled through Dave's submarine. Behind them, octopi pushed a cage holding the four North Wind agents.

"Remain calm! Do not panic! We will still win!" Short Fuse cried. Then he started to lose it. The poor little guy was bawling hard.

Kowalski reached through the bars to touch Eva. Her head spun around to look at him. All the fire was gone from her eyes.

"Eva! I know," Kowalski said sympathetically.

Agent Classified turned his head away. He felt just as bad as the others, but he wasn't about to show it.

Inside, though, the truth hurt.

For the first time, he had failed.

CHAPTER 16
Dave Wins!

Dave gasped in mock surprise as his hench-
men wheeled the penguin cage before him.

"Welcome! Skipper, Kowalski, and rootin-tootin'
Rico!" he said. "The gang's all here! The mood is
electric! Is that really finally everybody?"

His henchman Nicholas filled in the last portion
of their penguin chart. All of the octopi let out a
garbled cheer.

Skipper gripped the bars of the cage. "All right,
Dave. Just what have you done with—"

Before he could finish, Dave slipped around a
metal table with Private strapped to it.

"Private!" Skipper cried.

"Guys!" Private cheered. "You're in for it now, Dave!"

"Really?" Dave asked. He turned the ray toward Private. It was loaded with Medusa Serum.

"Now, who's ready to move into live penguin testing?" Dave asked.

"You move that death ray away from Private right now!" Skipper yelled.

"It's not a death ray, Skipper!" Private called out. "He's gonna turn us into monsters!"

Dave nodded. "Yepper-doo!"

"Skipper!" Private cried.

Skipper was horrified. "You can't take away Private's cuteness!"

"He's the cute one! That's his thing!" Kowalski said.

Rico nodded.

"What?" Private asked.

"It's all the little guy's got!" Skipper went on.

Private sighed. Is that really all his team thought of him? That all he could do was be cute?

Looking sad made him even more adorable.

"Hmm, you are supercute," Dave said, eyeing him. "We'd better crank this up."

He nodded to two henchmen.

"Drew, Barry, more power!" he commanded.

They quickly worked on the machine, and it hummed louder.

"Skipper?" Private asked nervously. "Any time now. . . ."

Skipper looked at Dave. "Your plan is insane! Do you really think any of this is going to make people love you?"

Dave held a tentacle over the Fire button. "No, but they'll despise you. Isn't that what really matters? Ready?"

"Negotiations have broken down," Kowalski said worriedly.

"Rico! The paper clip! Get us out of here!" Skipper ordered.

Rico coughed up a baseball glove.

"We need that paper clip. Chop-chop, soldier!" said Skipper frantically.

Kowalski slipped on the baseball glove and

started to catch the items that Rico coughed up. A toothbrush . . . a teddy bear . . . a sippy cup . . . but no paper clip.

Skipper got behind him, gripped him around the waist, and squeezed Rico's belly. "Where's the paper clip?"

He glanced over at Private. The ray inched closer and closer to the frightened little guy.

"No!" Skipper yelled.

Private looked over and saw Rico trying to cough up the paper clip. That reminded him of something—the paper clip he had swallowed earlier. He coughed and gagged.

Zap! Dave fired the ray. There was an explosion of green smoke.

"No!" Skipper wailed.

The smoke cleared, and Skipper rubbed his eyes. "Private?"

He looked at the table, expecting to see a monster there. But Private wasn't there. All that was left were a few feathers.

Dave looked confused. "I disintegrated him.

That wasn't supposed to happen."

Rico was devastated.

"You maniac! You blew him up!" Kowalski yelled.

"No . . . ," Skipper whispered.

Dave shrugged. "Oh well. This is why we test things, people. I'll have to lower the power for the others." He nodded to his henchmen. "Gentlemen, chart a course for New York City. The monsters are due in Manhattan."

Dave made an announcement over the sub's speakers. "All henchmen report to your posts."

A henchman rolled the penguins' cage away, and Dave followed. Skipper, Kowalski, and Rico wiped away tears. Private was gone . . . gone forever!

Or was he? Once the room was empty, a penguin appeared from behind the metal table. A really cute penguin, holding a paper clip. The paper clip that had unlocked him from the metal table just in time.

Private was alive!

CHAPTER 17
Saving the North Wind

Dave's henchmen quickly got to work. They chained together the North Wind agents and placed them on a platform in the Death Machine room. One of the henchmen, Brutus, stood behind a console, ready to activate the machine and destroy the agents.

"All right, octopus!" Agent Classified called out. "Whatever Dave's paying you, I'll double it!"

Brutus replied in garbled octopus speech.

"Is that a yes?" Classified asked. He looked at his team members. "Does anyone speak octopus?"

"Sorry," replied Eva.

"Nope," said Short Fuse.

"Not a clue," answered Corporal.

"Blast it!" Classified cried. He pointed at Brutus. "You. Free us," he said as if he were talking to a child. "We give you ma-ny fish-es."

Classified pantomimed eating a fish. "Mmm, yummy!"

Brutus ignored him. He punched buttons on the console, and the platform flipped around. An enormous death machine faced them.

"What is that?" Classified asked.

Bright lights came on, illuminating the dials on the death machine: Dead. Deader. Deadest. Really Dead. Really, Really Dead.

"Oh great," Classified moaned.

The machine whirred to life. The platform slowly inched toward the machine. *Whomp!* Two metal compactors slammed together. As soon as the platform reached them, they'd be crushed.

Whomp!

Short Fuse started to lose it again. "Oh no! This is it!"

"I don't want to die all squishy!" Corporal wailed.

Eva rolled her eyes. She was the only one who kept her cool.

The platform inched even closer. . . .

"Oh, we're dead! Dead! Dead!" Classified yelled, grabbing onto Corporal.

Suddenly, the team was whisked backward just before the compactors smashed together.

Whomp!

Classified's eyes were shut tightly. He didn't realize they'd been saved. "Oh no! We're dead! Deeeeeeeaaaaaaaaad!"

The platform revolved around, revealing Private at the controls, holding a bat. Brutus fell to the ground, unconscious.

Private pressed a button, releasing the chains binding the agents. Classified still clung to Corporal. When he opened his eyes and saw Private, he snapped back into tough-guy mode.

"Hello! I pushed a button!" Private said.

"Ho ho ho! Super! Well done, Private!" he praised.

"Good work, *malinki*," Eva said affectionately.

"Eh, yes, excellent button pushing," Classified said, trying to cover for his failure. "Hm. Compliment, praise, etcetera. All right agents, we are back in business. Time to take down Dave."

Private smiled, glad to be part of a team again. Then he saw the North Wind racing for the wrong exit. "Wait! Skipper, Kowalski, Rico—and those penguins," Private said, pointing. "They're this way!"

The agents stopped.

"Right, and as soon as we return to the North Wind headquarters, grab fresh equipment, and work up a smashing new plan, we'll come speeding back and take down Dave," Classified said.

"But they're in danger!" Private urged.

"We can't go running in without a plan," Eva said.

"We got no tech, man! I need my booms!" Short Fuse said.

Private was angry. "Skipper wouldn't care! Plan or no! Fancy equipment or no! He'd never leave a man behind!"

His words stopped the agents. They watched as Private, small and alone, took the exit leading toward danger. They hesitated for a moment—and then Classified led them through the opposite door.

"Come on," Classified said.

CHAPTER 18
Dave Takes Manhattan

Inside his submarine, Dave was getting ready for his big New York appearance. He spoke to his henchmen. "Gentlemen, what we do now, we do for all octopus-kind. But mostly for me." Dave looked up to watch a news report on his TV screen.

"BREAKING NEWS! The penguins have been found," the reporter was saying. "Okay, according to my notes, genetic researcher Dr. Octavius Brine has found the penguins and is bringing them here to New York's Battery Park. The penguins are coming back! Oh my gosh! Loooook!"

Dave suddenly appeared on the water, rising

from the unseen submarine below him. He held a microphone. He tapped it to make sure it was working and then said, "Penguin lovers of the world! Guess who I found?" The crowd roared with delight.

"It wasn't easy," Dave continued, "but seeing the penguins get what they deserve will make it all worthwhile."

"What a weird thing to say," the news reporter said. "I'm so excited!"

Dave turned to his henchman. "Do it," he ordered.

Back inside the sub, Private peered through a window at the pile of penguins. He tried to get the attention of his brothers.

"Skipper! Skipper! Rico! Kowalski!" he called out.

They could barely hear him over the triumphant music playing behind Dave.

"It's like I can still hear his little voice, calling to us," Skipper said.

"You have to get out of there!" Private yelled. "Move!"

"It's like he's saying, 'You have a great otter there. Moo,'" Skipper said.

"Why would he moo?" Kowalski asked.

"What are you asking *me* for?" Skipper replied. "I'm not Private's little ghost."

Then Brutus hit a button.

Zap! The ray beamed the Medusa Serum all over the captured penguins.

"Noooooo!" Private wailed.

CHAPTER 19
Mutants Unleashed!

Outside, the crowd couldn't wait to see their beloved penguins.

"Are you READY?" Dave asked the crowd.

"YEAH!" they cheered.

Dave walked down the side of the sub, laughing maniacally. "Yay! Your new and improved penguins!"

The mouth of the submarine tilted upward, shooting out a mass of penguins. Smoke billowed out along with them, spreading across the water and through the park.

The penguins landed in Battery Park and marched

through the park. Confused, the crowd tried to see them through the thick fog.

"Mommy, it's the penguins!" a little girl exclaimed, walking closer to the line of marching penguins.

Then the fog slowly cleared . . . revealing not a bunch of adorable penguins, but an army of mutant penguins! All their cuteness was gone. Now they looked really scary.

The former penguin-loving people started swatting at the mutant penguins with penguin backpacks and stuffed penguin toys. In a daze, the mutants swatted back at them, all grunting like Frankenstein's monster. The happy reunion became a free-for-all: humans against penguins, and penguins against humans.

Back in the submarine, Private peered through the periscope and watched the scene. This was terrible!

"Oh dear. Oh no. Oh no, oh no . . . ," he moaned.

Suddenly, Private heard a loud noise. "Crikey!" he said. He turned around just in time to see several octopi henchmen drop from the ceiling, trapping

Private in. He looked around. There was no way out, but he refused to let the henchmen think he was scared.

"Come on, then. You wanna go?" he shouted. "You want some argy bargy?" Then with a sudden burst of confidence, Private charged them. He let out a war cry. "Aaaaaagh!"

The octopi charged, and it looked like Private was doomed. But just as they were about to make contact, Private disappeared.

The octopi henchmen looked at each other in confusion. "Where'd he go?" one asked.

And then the octopi heard a familiar sound—the sound of the ray vehicle revving up.

"YAAAAAAAHHH!!!" Private yelled, as he crashed right through the henchmen. The octopi scattered left and right.

Dave didn't notice Private driving out of the sub, piloting the ray. Private quickly spotted mutant Skipper. With a crazed look in his watery eyes, Skipper was eating stuffed penguins from a souvenir stand. A terrified cat ran by, and Skipper grabbed it.

Private jumped down from the ray and ran to Skipper. "Skipper! Don't eat that!"

Skipper turned to look at Private.

"Gnagh!" he blurted out. His mind had been mutantized too.

"It's okay, Skipper," Private said. "It's me, Private."

Skipper lunged at him, but Private quickly dodged out of the way.

"I know you're in there somewhere," Private told him.

"Gnaghgnaghgnaghgnagh!" Skipper replied.

Skipper swung his giant flipper at Private. Now it had a wicked-looking claw at the end. Private dodged again.

"Listen! This isn't you!" Private told him.

Skipper paused. It looked like he was thinking it over.

Then he swallowed the cat.

"No! Bad Skipper!" Private yelled.

Skipper lunged for Private again. This time, Private didn't dodge him. Instead, he slapped Skipper across the face.

123

"Oh, dear," Private said. He would never dream of slapping Skipper. Not even a horrible, mutant, cat-eating Skipper. But now he had done it!

Skipper stared at Private. The slap jarred something in Skipper's brain. Images flashed through his mind. Baby Private, hatching from an egg. Private giving Skipper a silly salute. Private making an adorable sad face.

"Pry-vit?" Skipper asked.

"Yes! That's it!" Private said.

"Private! You're alive!" Skipper cheered in his normal voice.

Skipper's body was still mutant, but his brain was back to normal. He hugged Private, laughing and then sobbing.

Then he coughed, and the cat jumped out of his mutant mouth.

"Sorry," Skipper told Private. "It's just that I thought you were a goner."

Mutant Skipper and Private hurried to find the rest of their team. They spotted mutant Kowalski getting ready to throw a trash can through a store window. His flippers had transformed into tentacles! They ran up to stop him.

"*Urgh? Hissssssssssssss!*" Kowalski flailed his tentacles at them.

"Get a grip on yourself, soldier!" Skipper said. "That's an order!"

"He's not getting a grip!" Private pointed out.

"Wait! I'll speak Mutant Zombie Penguin to him!" Skipper said. He turned to Kowalski. "*Gerbitwaaahbuggahissss!*"

Kowalski paused . . . and threw the garbage can over Skipper and Private's heads.

Skipper shrugged. "Well, that's all I've got."

Kowalski menacingly slithered toward them.

Private thought quickly. "Kowalski, Eva is worried about you!"

Kowalski's mind instantly snapped back to normal.

"She is?" he asked.

Skipper patted Private on the shoulder.

"What did she say? Did she say my name specifically? Were there tears? Details!" Kowalski begged.

Then it hit him. "Private, you're alive! Come here!"

He hugged Private with his snaky flippers.

"This feels a little awkward, but I'm happy," he said.

Then they heard a familiar garbled cry, and turned to see Rico on a kebab cart. A pair of wings had sprouted from his back! He chased away the cart owner by waving a flaming kebab, and then swallowed the kebab like a sword swallower.

"*Graaagh!*" he yelled.

"Rico, you listen to us!" Skipper pleaded. "You're—"

Burp! Rico belched loudly and a puff of smoke came out. He smiled and waved.

"Eh, I guess you're kind of the same either way," Skipper realized.

Then Rico noticed Private. He leaped down from the kebab cart and tried to kiss Private with his mutant beak. Skipper quickly separated them.

"Save your hug for the holidays, Rico," Skipper told him. "We've got a mutant apocalypse to bring down!"

126

CHAPTER 20
Private's Sacrifice

Private quickly led them all to the ray.

"Private, you stole Dave's ray!" Kowalski exclaimed.

Private nodded. "Yeah! I thought we could use it to turn everyone back to normal." He handed the ray remote to Skipper.

Kowalski peered at the glowing green serum inside. "It's not that simple," he said. "To reverse the ray, we'd have to swap out the Medusa Serum with a fuel source of almost immeasurable cuteness."

"You mean, like, a chipmunk?" Skipper asked.

"Not cute enough, sir," Kowalski replied.

Skipper upped the cuteness. "Riding a train, in a cowboy hat?"

Kowalski shook his head. "No."

"Inside a Japanese girl's backpack?" Skipper tried.

"What part of 'immeasurable cuteness' do you not understand?" asked a frustrated Kowalski.

Private suddenly realized what he had to do. Maybe he wasn't a great leader, like Skipper. Or supersmart, like Kowalski. Or super . . . whatever Rico was. But he was cute. Really cute.

Immeasurably cute.

Without another thought, he hopped inside the ray and attached the cables to himself. Skipper spotted him.

"Hey! What are you doing?" Skipper yelled to Private.

"We have to change these penguins back before somebody gets hurt," Private said.

"No, wait. No, no, waaah!" Skipper yelled, and he dropped the ray remote. That triggered the ray. A beam hit a random penguin and turned her back to normal.

"The ray, it works! It WORKS!" Kowalski cheered.

"Private, are you okay?" Skipper asked nervously.

"Yes," Private answered. But Skipper, Kowalski and Rico all stared at him and gasped. Private had a butt-hand.

"Whoa, butt-hand! There's a hand attached to his butt. That was not . . . that was not there before!" Kowalski said. Private turned around to look and jumped, causing the cables to fall off of him.

"Get out of there! That's an order! This is too dangerous!" Skipper commanded.

"Permission to defy order!" Private replied.

"Permission denied," Skipper said.

"Then I deny your denial!" Private cried.

"He's gone rogue!" Kowalski said worriedly.

Skipper jumped up and grabbed onto the ray.

"Private, we don't know what this is going to do to you. It already made you sprout a butt-hand!" Skipper told him.

"Skipper, this is the mission I've been training for my entire life. I know it has to be me this time," Private replied. "And I think you know it too. *I'm* the secret weapon."

Private fired up the ray. Skipper looked out at the chaos all around them. Hundreds of poor, confused mutant penguins battling with terrified humans. Private was right. It had to stop—now. And Private was the one to do it. Reluctantly, he let go of the ray and dropped back down with Rico and Kowalski.

"I guess it's true what they say," he said, his voice filled with emotion. "There comes a time when you have to let a boy grow up and strap a tube to his head and his butt that uses his cuteness to power a ray that zaps mutants back to normal. I just didn't think it would be today."

He picked up the remote and raised the ray higher, so its beam could reach more penguins.

Across the park, Dave did a happy dance, stopping every few moments to kick a penguin into a person or a person into a penguin.

"La-la-la, boot!" he sang. "Tra-la-la, kick!"

Dave hopped on top of a souvenir stand to get a better view of the scene.

"Yes! Fear them! Hate them!" he cried.

Then he noticed the giant ray rising above the tree line.

"Are you kidding me?" he asked. "They're going to un-mutant my mutants! *Aaaaaaaaaaaaaah!*"

With a loud war cry, he ripped off his Dr. Brine costume and charged across the park. He barked orders to his octopus henchmen through a walkie-talkie.

"They're on the ray! Hunt them down! Hurt them! Bury them!" Then he turned to an octopus in a chef's hat. Kevin, bake on!" he ordered. "We're still going to need that victory cake."

Then he tossed the radio and headed for the ray. Skipper spotted him speeding toward them, his face red with fury.

"Uh-oh. I haven't seen anyone this angry since we all missed Rico's recital," Skipper said. "We only have time for one shot. What's the ETA, Kowalski?"

Up on the ray, Kowalski and Rico were busy taping snow globes together to make one giant snow globe disco ball. With it, they could split the beam from the ray so that it would hit every penguin in the park.

"Going as fast as I can!" Kowalski called back. "These tentacles are tricky!"

Rico added another snow globe to the ball, and Kowalski laid down another strip of tape over it.

Then Rico noticed a small army of octopus henchmen headed toward them. They had to fire now!

"Uh-oh!" Rico said, pointing.

"Octopi!" Private yelled.

"Nearly there!" Kowalski promised.

Rico grabbed Kowalski and flew down from the top of the ray.

"Beam splitter ready!" Kowalski reported. "Fire at will!"

Dave realized he wouldn't get to the ray in time. He knocked a kid off a playground merry-go-round. Then he wound his tentacles around the bars.

"Oh, I don't think so!" he yelled.

He used the spinning motion of the playground ride to launch himself into the air. At the same time, Skipper pressed the button on the remote.

Click. Click. Nothing happened. Then the no battery light flashed.

"Dead batteries?" Skipper couldn't believe it. "Batteries, Rico, we need batteries! Go, go, go!"

Rico raced off and found a Battery Park battery stand. But the sign on the front said SOLD OUT.

Rico spun around, noticing a convenience store on the edge of the park. He quickly flew through its doors, landing right next to the batteries . . . which were right next to a rack of Cheezy Dibbles!

At the same time, Skipper and Kowalski turned to face the octopus army. Kowalski jumped upside down on top of his huge, mutant head and wrapped his tentacles around himself. Skipper yanked one of the tentacles like a rip cord, sending Kowalski hurtling toward the henchmen like a spinning top.

Then a bunch of things happened at the same time:

Rico stood in the convenience store, trying to choose between regular and spicy Cheezy Dibbles.

Dave soared through the sky, headed right for the ray.

Skipper slid under the line of octopus henchmen, whacking them with the remote as he passed.

Then Rico coughed up the money (along with a harmonica and a rubber ducky) to pay for the batteries and the bags of Cheezy Dibbles and flew off. He tossed the batteries to Skipper.

Skipper caught the batteries and slammed them into the remote.

"Ha-ha!" Skipper cried triumphantly. He moved to press the button when . . .

Smack! A henchman reached Skipper and knocked the remote out of his flippers. It sailed out of reach.

"Nooooooooo!" Skipper wailed.

Kowalski dove for it but missed.

The remote flew through wiggling octopus tentacles as the henchmen tried to grab for it.

Skipper tripped, hit the ground, and bounced back up.

"Dibble me!" he yelled to Rico.

Rico tossed Skipper a bag of Dibbles. Skipper popped the bag, sending one lone Dibble shooting through the tangle of tentacles.

Squish! Dave smacked into the giant snow globe on top of the ray. He wrapped his tentacles around it and reached past it toward Private.

At the same moment, the lone Dibble reached the remote before the octopi could.

Dink! The dibble hit the big red button, and the ray fired with a tremendous burst of energy.

Then a brilliant flash of light blinded them all.

CHAPTER 21
A Valued Member of the Team

As the light faded, a purple octopus tentacle wrapped around a skyscraper. Dave laughed maniacally . . . and then bumped into an invisible wall. Catching his reflection in the plastic, he realized the truth.

Dave had not transformed into a giant, city-conquering octopus. He had transformed into an adorable, tiny octopus with a supercute face! And now he was trapped inside a snow globe.

"What?" Dave asked. "Are you monkey-fighting kidding me?"

He looked around the park. Soft, pink light

bathed the park, and hundreds of small, cute penguins began to dance around happily. The ray had worked! They were all back to normal!

Skipper, Kowalski, and Rico looked at one another and let out a cheer. They were back to normal too! Then a tumble of tiny, cute octopi henchmen fell on them. The ray had worked on them too.

Skipper, Kowalski, and Rico looked at the ray chamber, which was clouded in mist. They slowly approached. Was Private all right? "Private!" Skipper yelled.

"He's at stage eight on the mutation scale," Kowalski yelled. "And the scale only goes to five!"

A shell began to encase Private on all sides.

"Don't worry, a chrysalis is forming around you," Kowalski said to Private. "That's perfectly normal."

At this point Corporal stepped in to help. He smashed the glass chamber of the ray, and gently placed Private's chrysalis in front of Skipper.

"Private . . . ," Skipper whispered.

Just then the outer casing of the chrysalis began to crack.

Skipper, Rico, and Kowalski all gasped.

SPLAT! The shell exploded, covering everyone in goop.

"Private?" Skipper said cautiously.

Private was woozy. And he had a new mutation. His butt-hand was gone, but now a tiny chicken head had sprouted on top of his head!

"Hello," Private said.

"Hello!" the chicken head squawked.

The penguins all laughed and cheered, until Private's chicken head clamped down on Kowalski's head.

"Aaagh!" Kowalski yelled.

Private struggled with the chicken head until he finally managed to pull it off Kowalski.

"Hehe. Sorry," Private said.

Skipper was overcome with emotion. "Soldier, you apologize for nothing," Skipper told him. "You just saved our lives. Heck, you just saved the whole dad-blasted species! You're the best one of us all. You're the elite-est of the elite. The most meaningful and valued member of this team."

Private beamed and saluted Skipper, who saluted

right back. Then Skipper stuck his tongue out at Private, and he giggled. Then all the penguins rushed in for a group hug.

Tiny, cute Dave began screaming inside the snow globe. He started running like a hamster on a wheel, and rolled himself over to Skipper.

"Oooh, look at you!" Skipper says.

"You think this is over?" Dave said. "I'm just getting started. I'm going to mutate every cute creature in the world!"

Skipper saw the little girl who had been so scared by the penguins earlier. He tossed her the snow globe. She looked inside and smiled.

"Cool, an octopus!" she said.

Dave smiled back, glad to be wanted.

"I hope you find happiness, Dave," Skipper said kindly.

The girl began to shake the snow globe. "It's snowing! It's snowing! It's snowing!" she shouted.

"Aaaaaaaaaaah!" Dave wailed.

The penguins suddenly looked up as a loud sound roared overhead.

Classified turned to Skipper and his crew. Then he looked around the park. There was the little girl, shaking a snow globe with what looked like a tiny Dave inside it. There were some humans and penguins cuddling on a bench. Playing catch. Sharing an ice cream cone. Riding a bicycle built for two. He took it all in, stunned.

He cleared his throat. "Penguins, this is difficult for me to say, but—"

"Is it 'osteoporosis'?" Skipper asked. "You just gotta lean into the vowels. Ahhh-stee-ohhhh-pahhh—"

"What? No," Classified said. "I need to say that I was *wrong* about you. And there's only one way to make it right."

"Give us jetpacks," said Kowalski.

"We could kiss," said Eva at the same time.

Kowalski's eyes widened. Had he heard right?

"Whoa! Uh, did you just say—"

Eva grabbed him, dipped him, and lifted her wing to block everyone's view. Skipper covered Private's eyes. When Eva lowered her wing, Kowalski had kiss marks all over his beak.

"Well, that feels right!" he said, beaming.

"I think I'd actually prefer a jetpack, please," Private said.

Skipper turned to Classified. "You heard the man!" he said.

The next day, the penguins were all merrily soaring through the sky with their new jetpacks. Everything was great, except for one thing. Private still had a chicken head.

Private flew over to Skipper's side. "So, are we turning me back to normal, or . . . ?"

Skipper grinned. "Well, what is normal, Private? I believe we've learned from this delightful adventure that looks don't matter, it's what's inside that counts."

Kowalski flew over to join them. Private's chicken head suddenly grabbed onto Kowalski's head, ripped him out of his backpack and threw him away. Private gasped! Luckily, Rico caught

Kowalski in time and plopped him back in his jetpack.

"All right, fine. We'll turn you back first thing Monday," Skipper promised.

The penguins all cheered and zipped off on their jetpacks into the glorious future.